I0460621

THE QUEEN'S CHILDREN

Raymond Wemmlinger

SAPERE
BOOKS

THE QUEEN'S CHILDREN

Published by Sapere Books.

24 Trafalgar Road, Ilkley, LS29 8HH

saperebooks.com

Copyright © Raymond Wemmlinger, 2025

Raymond Wemmlinger has asserted his right to be identified as the author of this work.
All rights reserved.

No part of this publication may be reproduced, stored in any retrieval system, or transmitted, in any form, or by any means, electronic, mechanical, photocopying, recording, or otherwise, without the prior written permission of the publishers.
This book is a work of fiction. Names, characters, businesses, organisations, places and events, other than those clearly in the public domain, are either the product of the author's imagination, or are used fictitiously.
Any resemblances to actual persons, living or dead, events or locales are purely coincidental.

ISBN: 978-0-85495-723-1

1

"Her name," James said, for all to hear as he took his daughter in his arms for the first time, "is Mary."

There was an instant of surprised silence, before one incredulous voice rang out from the throng of courtiers packed into the room beyond the foot of my bed. 'Mary?' it echoed. But then came the burst of appropriate applause, and cries of 'God bless Princess Mary!' No doubt nearly all of them were shocked by James's choice, but after almost two years in England I was well familiar with the deftness of the English couriers in always managing a perfect response.

I leaned back on my pillows, grateful for their soft embrace after the rigours of the birthing chair. I was comforted by the beautiful bedroom, which was green and white with large windows that looked out onto the Greenwich Palace gardens and park. The birth had been my easiest, perhaps because of the greater efforts of the English doctors, who for months had fussed around me in ways their Scottish counterparts never had.

James carefully placed the infant back in my arms. "Thank you, Anne," he whispered, "for this beautiful child. And for the others still before us." His hooded blue eyes, after so many years still enigmatic to me, opened more than usual, so that the sincerity of his gaze was clear. They were still the eyes of a young man, which was fitting. At almost thirty-nine, he still looked as youthful as I did at thirty. His hair like mine was free of grey, although I expected his, not as fair as mine, would show it earlier. He also had the look of a man satisfied with life. If he felt any disappointment at the child being female, he was still grateful for her. The courtiers, too, had put a good face on it, and there'd been only the tiniest hesitation before the cheers when the midwife had announced it was a girl. Eagerness for a boy had been strong throughout not only the court but the entire country. But I had only wanted for the new child, boy or girl, to arrive healthy and strong, and it was with gratitude that I now held her. I was as confident as James that more would follow.

The crowd parted, allowing Henry, Elizabeth and Charles through, escorted by the Countess of Bedford, whose daily presence I now relied on. The children had each arrived more than a week ago from their various households, Henry's a short trip up the Thames at Hampton Court, Elizabeth's at Coombe Abbey, and Charles's in London. Charles, now four, was still not robust, and today held Henry's hand and hovered close to him as if intimidated by the crowd. With his dark hair and eyes and slender body, he looked different from his siblings, and James and myself. But fair-haired and blue-eyed Henry, at eleven, and Elizabeth, nearly nine, both tall for their ages, were the very portraits of good health and vitality. Both carried themselves with regal dignity and looked much alike, handsome and beautiful, except that Elizabeth's face mostly wore an expression of eager anticipation, while Henry's was one of serious restraint, and even a touch of sadness.

"Your new sister's name," James said as they approached the bed, "is Mary."

All three stopped where they were. A startled look crossed Henry's face before vanishing. But Elizabeth stared frankly at James and asked, "Mary?" Charles, too young to understand but still sensing a jarring note had been struck, shrank closer to Henry.

"Mary," I repeated reassuringly. I, too, had been surprised when James had told me he wanted to name her after his mother should the child be a girl, for Mary Queen of Scots had been a figurehead for the religious struggles in England. Another name would have been preferable to me, but I'd decided not to tell him. Such fears and superstitions were foolish, and couldn't possibly cloud the happiness we'd found since coming to England. I would not introduce any dark thoughts into our plans for the new child. And when Anna — the only one of my attendants that I ever shared my concerns with — had quietly replied that the name of the mother of our Lord could only bring further blessings, I'd known I'd made the right decisions.

James went to the still hesitant children and rested his hands lightly on their shoulders. He'd grown easier with them in England, especially with Henry and Charles, who he saw often because of the nearness of their households.

"Birth," he said, ushering them forward to the bed, "is a wonderful thing, especially the birth of a princess." Elizabeth smiled, but Henry's gaze became fixed. The look passed quickly, but it was enough to suggest that he remembered the last time I'd given birth, at Stirling Castle, and the accompanying discord and sad outcome. I sensed it was important for him to learn that not all births ended in the Stuart vault at Holyrood. "She is healthy and beautiful," I said with confidence. "A long life blessed by God is surely ahead of her."

Applause sounded in the room, now even more crowded with other courtiers who'd followed the countess and children in. Elizabeth laughed merrily and rested on the bed to see her little sister better. And finally, Henry smiled, in a way that looked reserved but genuine. With enthusiasm he lifted up Charles for a better view and said, "Our new sister."

The crowd had surged forward, but the countess stopped them, holding up her palms. With a quick glance at James for approval, she motioned to Anna, who went to a side door and let in the midwives and nurses to swaddle the tiny princess and lay her in her new cradle. A fortune had been spent on its green carnation velvet, silver trim and taffeta covers, its satin lining, and on cambric and lace baby gowns, as well as handkerchiefs and linens. The government had also approved funding for a huge number of attending staff. Almost seventy years had passed since the birth of an English prince or princess, and the anticipation had been widely felt.

As Mary was taken to the nursery, James addressed the courtiers again, before dismissing them. "My first daughter was named for my kinswoman Queen Elizabeth, who entered the world in this very room. It was through her grace and intention that I now occupy her throne. But the path to it was set by my mother. I name this child after her, as a sign of the peace and harmony we have attained. The strife and tensions of religion that tore this land during the day of the two queens are now behind us."

There was applause, but thinner than before. James didn't seem to notice. I wondered if it would have been thinner still, had there been more Catholics in the room.

A little later, after everyone had left and we were alone, the Countess of Bedford agreed the response had left much to be desired.

The chair that had been pulled up beside my bed for her was straight but upholstered with rich tapestry, and she leaned back comfortably. Her words were as strong and full of insight as ever. "Many Catholics were disappointed the treaty with Spain didn't include terms for tolerance," she said frankly.

She was one of few friends with whom I could be unguarded in my responses, and I now sighed heavily with exasperation. During his years on the throne of Scotland, James had studied the politics of England in expectation of being named as Queen Elizabeth's successor. When this came to pass, he almost immediately called for the cessation of English hostilities with Spain lingering from the Armada conflict. Embassy ties had been reestablished at once, although it had taken nearly a year to finalise a treaty. During that time many English Catholics had urged the Spanish king to advocate for their plight as part of the treaty, but without success.

"But they are still so much better off than they were when Elizabeth was queen!" I said. "James has made it clear they can practise their religion so long as they do so quietly."

"Some want more. Those who harboured hopes for it now see there isn't going to be. A year ago, the naming of a princess for a Catholic figurehead would've been taken as a good sign. But now they know not to see it as more than it is."

"And what do you imagine that would be?" Although often I could understand James's decisions, this one had confused me.

The countess cast down her dark eyes as she thought. "Reclaiming his mother from the Catholics," she then said very precisely. "Matters have worked out nicely for him since coming to England. He may be feeling generous about her, and may have decided the Catholics were responsible for her downfall. Who wouldn't want to believe their mother was manipulated by others rather than deficient in herself?"

But if James was ready to so absolve his mother, I wasn't. "I've come to doubt the sincerity of her religious beliefs," I said disapprovingly. "Unfortunate experiences have taught me

I'm not skilled in politics, but I can still see it was opportune for her to align with the Catholics to give herself the best chance of gaining the English throne — or so she thought. The crown of Scotland wasn't enough for her and she wanted more. Her choices — and her ambitions — were her own, no matter how others made use of them. And I do not believe it was love that prompted her to marry either Lord Darnley or Lord Bothwell. It was ambition, always. If James is more kindly disposed to the memory of his mother now, I'm not. But I've no objection to his trying to detach that memory from the Catholic cause."

"Some English Catholics hoped his memory of her might emerge more strongly once he became king here," said the countess. "Or, that it had already, and he might have become a secret Catholic. Once they saw he favoured the Reformed Anglican Church here, they turned their hopes towards you."

Indeed, they had. I'd been approached secretly by the ambassadors and agents of foreign Catholic powers, and the Vatican. Even the Pope had sent me a rosary, which, although Anna had begged for it, I'd at once given to James. My involvement in politics in Scotland, religious or otherwise, had never succeeded, and in England I stayed out of it. The culture of the new Stuart court had become my domain, and my goal was for it to find respect throughout Europe. There was so much more money for us in England. James said that coming here had been like exchanging a bare simple bed for a luxuriously comfortable one with abundant pillows and cushions. Wealth we had only dreamed of in Scotland was available for art and dance and theatre. Poets, musicians, playwrights and artists had flocked to court seeking my patronage, and the English courtiers had been dazed by spectacular and elaborate entertainments. I'd had notable and satisfying success; I felt important in ways I never had in Scotland, and had no desire to become involved in politics.

There had been but one time, and one time only, I'd considered doing so, when a future marriage between Henry and the Spanish king's daughter had been proposed during the treaty negotiations. It had appealed to me, for it would bring a status few other marriages, if any, could. The Spanish royal family were Hapsburgs, of impeccable lineage, and controlled much of Europe. Spain's wealth poured in from mines in Mexico and Peru, its galleons arriving in China with silver and returning crammed with silks, porcelains, spices and all manner of goods commanding a fortune in Europe.

"The Catholics' best hope was in the plan for a future marriage between Henry and the Infanta," I told the countess. "I favoured the match, and I believe it appealed to James as a way of fostering his cherished goal of creating peace in Europe. It was unfortunate their terms were so unacceptable." The Spanish had insisted upon Henry being educated in Spain and raised a Catholic, which had terminated discussions.

"Perhaps it can be considered again later," the countess suggested. "When Parliament and the English Anglicans become more used to peace with Spain, and the Spanish are more tractable. And you have other children — a Spanish match might be arranged for one of them."

"No!" I grasped the gold- and silver-fringed edge of the embroidered bed cover. "Such a marriage has to be reserved for Henry. He is my firstborn, which makes him special not only to the kingdom but to me as his mother. None of my other children can ever hold the same place for me or mean as much." I stopped, remembering the countess had lost all her own children. There were things I couldn't say to a childless woman, especially one without a son. I couldn't say that Henry

11

was like a part of me that could be what I could not. Instead, I said, "Daughters merely repeat their mothers as they grow."

The countess smiled a little sadly, suggesting that her thoughts had indeed gone to her own losses. But I knew she held no resentment. She valued her friendship with me and took pride in being my confidante. "The daughter born to Anne Boleyn in this very room went on to reign as well as any king. Prince Henry is a child most queens dream of having and few do. But do not forget your daughters, and that you have another son."

"Charles is a disappointment," I said flatly. It was the first time I'd ever admitted I felt so, even to myself. "The contrast with Henry and Elizabeth makes it so noticeable. He doesn't even look like them, or this new child. I see nothing of myself or James in him. He is weak."

"Bodily strength can come," the countess began reassuringly. "He has improved since coming to England, and —"

"He was slow to speech also," I interrupted. Having finally acknowledged what I hadn't for so long, I wasn't going to retreat from it so easily. "At least he has the capacity for clear thought. But I have small hopes for him."

Her face changed subtly in a way I'd never seen before. She did not look critical but did not seem to sympathise with me. "None of us can understand how it is to be queen," she said eventually.

I let go of the bedcover fringe as I suddenly felt a deep loneliness. I looked past the countess to the windows behind her, knowing I had no words to explain it. "I wish these rooms were on the other side of the palace, by the Thames. The river connects Greenwich to everyone and everything in the kingdom, and other kingdoms too, after it flows out to the ocean. On this side, I feel remote from it."

"But the gardens and parks on this side are so lovely. Especially now it's April." The countess returned to our discussion of Henry. "The Spanish match may not be impossible. You may be able to discuss it again a little later. But for now, the king must assure the Anglicans that the Catholics aren't going to recruit, and can live quietly until they fade away. But Henry is young yet, and there is time until the matter of his marriage must be decided."

She was right. I would have to bide my time. Past experience had taught me that everything turned out right when I did. And although I could not seek it openly, I might be able to find a way to quietly initiate a path towards the future marriage. Meanwhile, it comforted me to remember that when Henry was king, he would have the rooms in the palace that James currently occupied, overlooking the Thames, whether married to the Spanish Infanta or not.

2

Over the following month, Elizabeth and Charles and their retinues left for their own residences, but Henry remained and accompanied us when we changed to the Tower in London. A lioness in the menagerie there had recently given birth, and he wanted to see the cubs.

We seldom stayed in the Tower's royal apartments, but I'd requested it, to immediately follow Mary's departure for her own new home. Although I had years ago reconciled myself to the necessity of separation from my children, it still saddened me, and I wanted a distraction. Staying there would allow me to visit the nearby Royal Exchange, with its remarkable shops full of expensive fine wares from all over the world. And, during the past month, I'd decided there was one purchase in particular I wanted to make.

The day we left Greenwich, it was overcast but without rain as our barges proceeded up the Thames, the gloominess of the weather offset by the usual excitement of the activity accompanying our changes of residence. Since Mary had left, I'd suffered intermittent bouts of weeping, consoled only by the knowledge that I had taken particular care in selecting the six rockers who went with her. I'd chosen women with kind faces and manners, who I could be confident would hover protectively and soothe her with the gentlest of rocking when she stirred in her cradle. It also comforted me to know her new home was not so far away, fifteen or so miles from London, easily reached for a visit. Already I was planning my first, in two months, after her swaddling had been removed.

As I sat in the barge in the centre of the small fleet making its way to London, I took comfort in Henry's presence beside me, beneath the royal canopy. I wondered if James had agreed to have him stay longer because he knew how difficult the time would be for me. He was certainly aware Henry was the child I was most attached to.

Henry seldom initiated conversation, so I was surprised when he said thoughtfully, "There are eleven lions at the Tower now. It's very rare for there to be four in a litter. None of the keepers expected it, even the oldest ones with most experience. Some have been there for a very long time — one even since the reign of King Henry."

"Those keepers must be very wise in their ways, then. Although sadly, my son, wisdom doesn't always accompany age. Sometimes yes, as the follies of youth are put away. But other times not, when the bitterness and rigidity of disappointment take over one. It's different for everyone."

He frowned pensively. "You mean those who expected things that never happened? I suppose you never know everything that awaits one in life. But every year I see better what is to come for me."

"So is the way of it for one fortunate enough to be a prince."

He started to say something but, surprisingly, stopped. He'd been taught early on that in his position he needed to show care when he spoke, and whenever he did it was always with measured and considered words, and he usually paused before answering a direct question. It was rare for him to change his mind after starting. Now, in the silence that replaced his intended words, I distinctly felt he had been about to disagree with what I'd said. I wondered with disbelief if it were possible that he didn't see himself as fortunate in being the son of a king. But before I could question him, he began to speak about the menagerie again. "There's a tiger there also, and a leopard, two pumas, and a jackal. But most of all, I want to see the cubs."

He turned his intelligent face towards me and smiled unconvincingly. He had returned to the subject of the animals to distract me from what he'd thought I'd noticed. Briefly, I wished we were merely an ordinary mother and son instead of a queen and a prince who needed to be so careful of their words, even with each other.

"When you are older you can have your own menagerie, with even more animals," I said. "As a prince, and then a king, you're going to have opportunities available to few. In a few years you'll have your own income, and some autonomy in what you do. You can build an entire new zoo for yourself, if you want."

His smile remained fixed and he made no reply. This time I couldn't tell at all what he was thinking. And I couldn't remember when the last time had been that I'd seen him smile with sincerity and spontaneity — or if I ever had. "When you're older you can do more of what you want," I repeated, but felt confused that it had sounded like an apology.

Ahead of us in the barge, the oarsmen rowed with steady and lulling repetition. Nearby the Countess of Bedford and two other gentlewomen sat side by side, all absorbed in their own thoughts. I quietly drew Henry's attention to them, saying, "They look to be the Three Fates. All they need is a spindle and thread." He was already studying the classics, and the Greek myth of one's destiny being measured out at birth by a thread would be known to him.

There was the expected pause before he answered, "Spun, measured, and snipped. Your life is laid out for you."

"It's only a myth," I said reassuringly, nudging his arm and giving a little laugh. It then became my turn to attempt to distract him with talk of the menagerie. "You might even have an elephant in your menagerie! I've heard tell of there once having been one."

"A gift from the King of France," he said knowingly. "A special house was built for it. But it didn't live more than a few years. They didn't know what to feed it. It's said they gave it wine to drink every day." He lifted his hand and with two fingers imitated a pair of scissors closing. "Snip," he said, without expression.

The Tower wharf was already crowded when we docked, with courtiers, staff and servants from James', Henry's and my retinues, while barges loaded with baggage floated further off in the river. James, who had gone ahead in his own barge, met us there. After patiently enduring the Mayor of London's formal welcome to the city, we crossed a drawbridge into the Outer Ward. There, James led us left towards the Lion's Tower, where the menagerie was. "To the lions," he ordered, "without delay. My son has been eager to see them and I would have his patience rewarded. We must pay tribute to the great lioness and her new cubs!" As though in response, several lions within roared almost in unison, drawing startled exclamations from the courtiers who had followed us. Turning around, James waved them away. "Leave us. Too great a crowd could agitate them. We're observing today, not hunting."

At the entrance he told our immediate attendants to remain outside.

Inside was a small courtyard with several barred cages opening to it. Some were empty, their open low rear gates suggesting caves the occupants had retreated into. But in others, the magnificently ferocious-looking beasts, some sitting still, others steadily pacing, stared out at us appraisingly. Suddenly I felt apprehensive, if not actually fearful. Although I had seen the lions before from a distance, I had never been so close to their cages. But the bars looked strong, and the many guards alert and vigilant, ready to use their weapons if needed.

The Keeper of the Menagerie, a surprisingly slight middle-aged man with prematurely greying hair, came forward, lithely bowing to each of us. "Your Majesties wish to see the new cubs?" he asked. His manner was straightforward and respectful but not overly deferential, unlike most of our courtiers. He wore a plain doublet and breeches that looked sturdy, likely of linen, clothes I imagined would be worn by everyday labourers. The contrast with James's rich satin with lace trim couldn't have been starker. But if I'd been asked right then which of the two men seemed more powerful, it would have been difficult to answer. There was a certainty in the Keeper's manner that told me he had the knowledge and experience to ensure our safety among the beasts, something that gave me more confidence than the bars of the cages or the swords of the guards.

"The cubs," James answered, "but their mother too. The lioness." He was already looking beyond the keeper to the cages.

"They're together," said the keeper. "This way." Escorting us to one of the cages, he went on, "You must stay several feet back. Visitors in this section are unusual. But it does allow a closer look." It was strange to hear someone so directly telling us what to do. He pointed to where we should stand, then on one side inconspicuously but firmly placed himself between us and the cage, without obstructing our view. A halberd-bearing guard took the same position opposite him.

Inside, the gate to the inner den was closed. Halfway between it and the front bars reclined the lioness, her four cubs tumbling and stalking each other around her. They were yellow like their mother, but had darker spots interspersed all over. The lioness seemed almost bored as she tolerated her offspring's antics, sometimes lazily swatting at one, or gently biting it. For a while, we all simply watched them, enchanted by the delightful scene before us.

"How surprising," James observed. "Their eyes look blue." Bizarrely, I thought of James's blue eyes, and mine, and Henry's and Elizabeth's. Mary's eyes promised to be blue, although it was too early to tell. Charles's alone were brown.

The keeper replied that such was the case with all cubs. "In a month or so they'll go to green, and then brown, like their parents. And the dark spots on their coats also fade."

James looked at Henry, who had been standing very still and staring at the cubs as though spellbound. "Do you find them as expected?" he asked.

An instant passed, and then another. Even the surrounding lions in their cages seemed to await Henry's response. Then he said, "Things of childhood fade away."

It was not at all what I thought he would say. But James only placed a hand on his shoulder and led him away, saying, "Come, let us see some of the other beasts here."

The keeper and guard with the halberd turned also. But Henry, beside me, stayed in place just long enough to stretch his hand towards the cage. Only I saw it, and I managed to pull him back by the sleeve before he reached through the bars.

The next day, the bells of the Royal Exchange announced my arrival as my coach approached. The streets along the way had been lined with cheering citizens who were still pleased I had presented them with another princess. As we reached the impressive columned entrance, I was taken over by a giddy anticipation. Because public commercial activity was unbefitting for a queen, my visits there were rare, but they always evoked memories of my childhood in Denmark. The style of the building was Flemish, not Danish, but it looked European in a way London did not, and whenever I entered the cloistered walkway of the large centre courtyard, I felt transported to a world very different from mine. Even the regal and imposing statue of a dour Queen Elizabeth was only a brief, sobering reminder of the formality of my life as queen. Other statues lining the edge of the steeply pitched roof, of cheerful and satisfied-looking merchants, were more in keeping with the lively activity of the exchange.

The courtyard walkways were crowded with merchants, the owners of shops and their staff, bankers and their clerks, and traders — a mix of Englishmen and foreigners who came to conduct business there. Although held at a distance by our guards, all cheered and applauded as I passed by with my preferred goldsmith, Mr. Heriot, who'd met me at my carriage. He had followed me and James to England, and thrived as we had, his fabulous jewellery and trinkets always in demand by courtiers and wealthy Londoners. Now in his middle years, his fair hair was as yet without grey, and his brown eyes still had the same sensitive look they'd had when I'd first met him in Scotland. If the more sophisticated and commercial culture of England had affected him, and his greater success here as a financer, he had retained the artist's soul directing his talent. The only sign of the social status his wealth had brought was the simple but unmistakably expensive black damask coat reaching all the way to his feet.

"Your Majesty," he said as he led me, followed by my women, past the crowd. "You grace the exchange by your visit here today."

"I should visit from time to time. In many ways the Royal Exchange is the centre of England, is it not?" The remark flattered the nearby crowd, and the applause continued as he ushered us into the building.

On the second floor were the legendary shops of the two or three other goldsmiths, as well as armourers, milliners, haberdashers, and traders selling trinkets, toys, and books. There were also apothecaries, perfumers, and shops selling all manner of exotic sweets that customers could linger over at small tables, after which, refreshed and refortified, they could resume their shopping. Some wares were on display in the long corridor, under the watchful eyes of attendants, while others could only be glimpsed through wide open doorways as we passed. The colours, scents and sounds were wondrously strange and different from those at any of the palaces.

Mr. Heriot's shop was prominently and centrally placed. Inside he escorted me to a thronelike chair, incongruous in the otherwise plainly furnished room, a contrast to the corridor we had entered from. For all its grandeur the chair was a little uncomfortable, and had clearly only been brought in for my visit. Nothing in the nearly empty room was meant to distract customers from the beauty of possible purchases.

"Shall I bring out some of our latest creations?" Mr. Heriot asked. "Would you prefer jewellery or trinkets?"

I waved away all my women except Anna; they retreated to an adjacent room where jewellery would be shown to them. "Mr. Heriot, I can never resist seeing anything you think may be of interest. You know my taste well and can choose. But first, I have a specific request for a gift I plan to make." I beckoned to Anna, who came forward with a small item wrapped in silk.

"This is a miniature portrait of myself." I gestured, and she gave it to him. "I would like it set in a locket appropriate as a fine gift. The locket itself must be encrusted with diamonds, while the chain can be of pearls, or whatever other gems you would find attractive. You can be imaginative. My only stipulation is that it looks as expensive as it is."

He examined the portrait. "It is quite a fine piece of work, although it still fails to capture the full beauty of the original."

The flattery was obligatory, even from someone I'd known for so many years, and I ignored it. "Seeing my image surrounded by gems of value may help the owner equally value the friendship."

"I assume the recipient of this gift is already chosen? Knowing who it is intended for helps in creating a design guaranteed to appeal."

"The Spanish ambassador. Mr. Heriot, as you are aware, I do not like it known when you are preparing a gift at my request. But should you be placed in a situation where you find it necessary to mention it, feel free to say it is in thanks for his efforts in arranging the treaty with England last year." As the Countess of Bedford had reminded me, although negotiations for a future marriage between Henry and the Infanta had failed, there was nothing to prevent them being returned to in the future. Since my conversation with her, I had decided it would be wise of me to begin to create a path towards it now.

"The choice of your portrait provides a personal touch," said Mr. Heriot. "I can shape a beautiful setting for it. Both you and the ambassador are sure to be pleased with it."

"Then we are agreed for you to proceed. As usual, please send the finished work to me for inspection." I leaned back in the chair, satisfied. "Now, let me see what else you have here that I might want." The giddiness I'd felt earlier returned, and I gave a little laugh. "Although in truth, I would likely want everything you have. But I must be selective in my purchases. The king's birthday approaches, and I'd like to find a gift for him."

"I believe I have just the thing." Mr. Heriot went to an inner door, opened it and spoke briefly to someone inside. As I waited, I listened to the excited chatter of my women in the next room as they pored over and tried on what must have been an array of beautiful rings, necklaces and bracelets. In a few minutes I would join them and make selections for them, and for myself. Today I was in the mood to see diamonds and pearls.

Mr. Heriot came back and offered me refreshment, which I declined, not wanting to risk appearing in a possibly soiled gown before the crowd I would pass on my way out. To prevent him offering it again I changed the subject, asking how he found life in England.

His head moved from side to side. "I do find some of the English different."

"Of course. We all do, but in various ways, depending on how we are involved with them. How do you find them as customers?"

"Many are the same as in Scotland. But England is a land of much greater wealth. There are those here whose fortunes have changed them in ways I rarely encountered in Scotland. And the changes are not for the better."

There was a dark note to his answer, and a part of me felt it would be better not to pursue it. But still, I asked, "What do you mean?"

"Most who seek what I offer want gifts to reward others, or to show them a sign of love or affection," Mr. Heriot explained. "Sometimes it is for themselves, and even then, the expression is a good one, a part of the beauty and joy of life. But there are others who seem to have endless voids they are trying to fill. Their desire for jewels and trinkets, or huge loans of money which they want for investment to gain more, is an almost desperate need to make up for an absence in their lives. What is missing for them is love. And sadly, Your Majesty, I find more of these unfortunate men and women here in England. But I suspect this is a trait that might have been more prevalent in Scotland had there been as much wealth there as here. My associates in the richest countries on the continent all tell me they have encountered the same."

I already knew the truth of what he said, but I had never articulated it. There was something very sad and disturbing about hearing it said aloud. The emptiness of the décor of the room we were in, intentional for commercial reasons, started to seem even more pronounced, the voices of my women in the adjoining room very far away. I wished Mr. Heriot would say something further, but he didn't, his sad smile a lingering epilogue to his words. An odd, indefinable fear began to come over me, but I shifted it to irritation that his gloomy observations should interfere with my enjoyment of the visit. I had, after all, asked no more than an idle question regarding how he found life in England, and it hadn't warranted such a ponderous reply.

Fortunately, one of the assistants appeared right then, with the suggested gifts. For James, he held out a small, locket-sized golden book with a chain of gold. It was beautifully detailed, with the edges of pages on the sides, and the cover and spine showing intricate leatherwork.

"How charming," I said appreciatively as I took it from him and held it closer. "But why is there no title? There would have been sufficient room for one to be engraved, albeit in tiny letters."

"That, Your Majesty, is the mystery of the piece. Perhaps it means one never knows what knowledge one is about to find in life. Something the king, as a man who prizes knowledge, is bound to appreciate."

The room around us no longer seemed so empty. My fingers closed around the little book. "Yes, Mr. Heriot, for certain."

3

In October I missed my monthly flow and suspected I was once again with child. My women were all sworn to secrecy until I knew for certain. During the first week of November, when the familiar morning nausea began, I was sure of it.

"James is going to be delighted," I told Anna. "This comes at a time I find very opportune. Something has been troubling him these past few days, and the good news should provide relief from whatever it is."

Ever since his return to Whitehall Palace from his hunting lodge at Royston, it had been clear something unsettling was preoccupying his thoughts. Typically, he relied on his intellect, rather than feelings, to solve important problems, whether for himself, his family, or his subjects. The deeper the matter, the deeper he would withdraw, considering it until he'd arrived at a plan. In the past days there'd been telltale signs of it, his usual restlessness being even more pronounced. He had difficulty sitting in repose, continually shifted in his seat, and paced more frequently, his fingers twisting his rings. He'd been unable to remain in prolonged conversation with me, as though constantly being drawn back to the overriding issue within. He also hadn't lingered after dinner and supper with the courtiers for entertainments or games as I and my women had, nor had he walked in the great garden at Whitehall with us.

There had been other indications of a matter of importance being at hand. Yesterday I had been notified that the Opening of Parliament, set for today and which I was to have attended along with James, Henry and Charles in a symbolic display of a stable royal family, had been delayed. In the palace more couriers than usual were coming and going, and many members of the Privy Council had arrived the previous day and remained for hours. I had even thought I'd noticed more guards about. But of that, I could not be sure, for I seldom paid attention to such things, especially since coming to England. Daily life felt calmer than it had in Scotland. Rather than notice the presence of guards, I was more apt to observe what courtiers were present, and what they wore.

As my women helped me dress, I told Anna I would hear morning prayers privately in my own chapel, and breakfast alone rather than accompany the rest of my household to the Dining Halls, as I usually did. "But please send a message to the king to come to me shortly after," I added. "He should hear the news about the child from me, before it reaches his ears another way." All of my attendants had noticed the nausea this morning, and they knew what it meant. They were devoted to me, but it was impossible to prevent court gossip. It was fortunate the Opening of Parliament had been delayed; the most important men in the kingdom would have been present, and had the nausea overtaken me there, my condition would have been apparent to all.

"Perhaps today isn't the best time to ask for him," Anna said hesitantly. Her tone gave me pause. Although still as much a friend as she'd been when she'd left Denmark with me, I confided in her less since coming to England. I still had not forgotten the time when, knowingly or not, she had advised me poorly because she'd been so influenced by her Catholic beliefs. Ever since then she had only offered opinions with reluctance. If she now did so, it must have been important.

We had been similar in age and looks when she'd accompanied me to Scotland so many years ago. But now her hair was already grey, and thinner, and though her face was still unlined, it was narrower. She seemed less defined to me, less substantial as a person. She had never wanted to marry; her life had been devoted to me and my family, and the quiet, secretive practice of her Catholic religion.

When I was dressed, I sent the other women away and asked her why I should not send for James.

"The king never retired last night," she answered. "He has been with the Privy Council since yesterday."

"So whatever problem he's been contending with has likely come to a head, and might soon be resolved. Yes, I should wait to tell him. I don't want his satisfaction at the personal news being lost within matters of state."

She looked at me oddly, and I knew she was thinking that for a queen there was little difference between personal and public matters.

"I should wait to tell him," I repeated. "Thank you, Anna, for reminding me. And it's likely I might not even see the king at all today."

But later in the morning James came to my rooms, arriving unexpectedly through the corridor entrance rather than the one directly connecting his rooms with mine. As soon as he entered, I saw that something was very wrong. Although in Scotland he had been indifferent about his grooming, he'd understood that in English society it mattered greatly, and so submitted to the ministrations of his valets in a daily routine. But this morning, he was dishevelled. A long brown robe, with expensive buttons and fringed borders, had been hastily thrown over his stained shirt and wrinkled doublet and hose, garments he'd clearly been wearing for much longer than usual. His hair and beard were uncombed.

At once, I dismissed my attendants. As they scurried out, he remained in the centre of the room, pacing back and forth and clutching the edges of the robe. Once the door had closed and we were alone, I drew closer to him and saw a remoteness in his expression, and a weariness beyond what would be expected of a man who'd not retired the night before.

"What has happened?" I asked as I reached him. I felt slightly nauseous again, but this time I wasn't sure if it was from concern or being with child.

The remote look on his face receded somewhat, and his body seemed to relax a little. One hand let go of the edge of the robe, and reached out and touched one of mine, as though for reassurance. Then he turned and went to the closed door my attendants had just departed through, leaning back against it.

"They meant to kill us, Anne." His voice was low and strangely empty of emotion.

"Kill us?" My anxiety sharpened; with effort, I dulled it enough to ask, "Who exactly was supposed to die?"

Both of his hands pressed back against the door. "Me," he answered, his voice barely more than a whisper. His eyes closed, and he added, "And you, and Henry and Charles."

My reply came quickly, and without thought. "Not Henry!"

He opened his eyes and looked at me, and I instantly knew it had been the wrong thing to say. It would drive a wedge between us for him to think my concern was more for Henry than him.

At once I sought to soften my response by reminding him of what we shared. "Not our children, James — the part of us that lives on after we are gone from this world! The dynasty we are founding!"

He blinked and leaned forward, a movement that somehow conveyed that I had altered my mistake in time. The ghost of

Mary Queen of Scots, and her rejection of her husband after the birth of her child, had once again been banished.

But other parts of the distant past were still in his thoughts. "Gunpowder, again," he said. "The conspirators were to have used gunpowder, just as it was used against my father." Lord Darnley's assassination was supposed to have happened in the explosion of the house where he'd stayed in Edinburgh. He'd escaped it, only to be strangled in the yard behind.

"But what has that to do with us, James?" I asked. "It was so long ago."

His fingers fluttered, and he began walking across the room, as he did when in thought. I felt easier, for it was his usual manner returning. Then, he said in a clear voice, "There has been a plot to assassinate us, along with everyone else at Parliament this morning. Thirty-six barrels of gunpowder were discovered under the House of Lords."

I could only stare at him, neither able nor wanting to comprehend what he'd said. Surely, he was wrong. All the time there was misinformation in reports. One needed to be careful about believing everything presented to one, especially if it seemed beyond the realm of possibility, as this was. I wanted to say so, to ask him why with his always analytical thinking, he'd been so ready to believe something that couldn't happen. But then I remembered Anna had told me the Council had been present overnight. This wasn't only James's interpretation of the situation.

Reaching the window at the far wall, James paused as though looking out, then turned to me. "It would have been death for all of us, Anne. Me. You. Our sons. All the officers and lords of the kingdom." He began pacing again, retracing his steps. "It's always been gunpowder," he said as he passed me. "While still in my mother's womb, a gun was pointed at me."

Scottish nobles had murdered the Queen of Scots' secretary, preventing her intervention by pointing a gun at her. I said, "That gun was pointed at your mother, and at you within her only to remind her of what she had to lose. It was her own folly that brought you both to such a place." A wave of nausea reminded me of my own condition. The thought of a pistol pointed at me in the final months of my pregnancy was unimaginable. I suddenly wanted nothing so much as to lie down on my bed. But I stood where I was. For a queen, troubles should not prompt retreat.

"I do not understand why such has been my fate," James replied.

"It has not been your fate," I protested. "Are we not still here now?"

"We are," he acknowledged. He was silent and still, but then came and took my hand, leading me to a chair by the windows. "Forgive me for having kept you standing." I sat and gestured for him to take the chair beside me, but he did not.

"I should have begun by telling you that the worst of the danger is past. But my mind is not so clear after so little sleep these past nights. Forgive me for such a lack of consideration."

I waved my hand dismissively. "Are you safe? Shouldn't guards have accompanied you here? And everywhere you go in the palace?"

"They are in the corridor."

"And are our children safe?"

"Their security was quietly ensured at their various homes when I first learned of a plot, upon my return from Royston. Our own here at Whitehall, also. But it does seem that the only violence was intended to take place at Westminster. In time, more is surely to be revealed. We have only questioned one man so far, a fellow found last night with the gunpowder during the search. He calls himself John Johnson, but it is unlikely that is his real name. He is, of course, a Catholic."

I said nothing. I now saw that I had been naïve to believe that the religious tensions throughout the nation were being pacified.

"A Catholic," he repeated. "And a very self-righteous one. I questioned him myself this morning. He didn't hesitate to say to me directly what he'd already admitted — that he had intended to destroy all of us, and regretted that he had failed. He was, he said, doing the work of God." James rarely sneered or expressed outright disdain for anyone, no matter how foolish he thought them. But now it was plain on his face. "Such men convince themselves God uses them for his purposes," he said. "In truth, it is they who are attempting to use him for their own. Most are dissatisfied with their lot in life."

"Did he implicate others?" I could only hope no earls or barons were involved. It would be fortunate for all of us if the plot was limited to a small fringe group of unhappy men who failed to understand that such action would not help the English Catholics at all.

"Not yet. He insists he was alone, but that is clearly impossible. One letter was found on him, addressed to a Guy Fawkes, which he says is one of his aliases. More should be revealed as the questioning continues."

He exhaled sharply, and then finally came and sat beside me, carefully arranging the folds of his robe about him. An unexpected look of contentment came over his face, as though he were satisfied with the steps he'd taken to maintain order. He even managed to smile at me as he said, "It's only a matter of time now until everything is right again. In the meantime, for your own safety I must ask that you remain here in your suite, until more of this plot has been understood."

For a moment, I thought I would faint. Breathing deeply, I steadied myself. The danger had passed, but I was taken with a feeling that something was still not right. Henry's face floated into my thoughts, and then that of Elizabeth, and then Charles — the order of appearance because of their age, I told myself, and not because of which I loved most. "Would it not be better to have our children brought here also? None of their homes is a fortress and they might easily be targeted."

"It is safer for us to be separated. I have thought you might be better off away from London. Would you prefer being at one of our other homes? Perhaps Greenwich Palace?"

The comforts of Greenwich appealed, as I knew I could expect the nausea to last for several weeks if not longer, and a quieter residence would have been preferable. But I would not for an instant consider leaving. In the short time James had been sitting with me, he had steadied himself. He needed me near him.

"The place of a queen is at the side of the king. I will stay here with you," I answered.

I knew without his saying so that he appreciated it.

4

I spent the next few days playing trivial games with my women while the other conspirators revealed by Guy Fawkes — the real name of John Johnson — were captured or killed in Warwickshire, where they'd fled. I then received a visit from the Secretary of State.

Although Robert Cecil was the most important man in England after James, our paths had as yet barely intersected, as I had little to do with matters of state. When the message came that he wished to see me, at first I almost said no, for the nausea from being with child was still with me. But then I decided to receive him in one of my formal reception rooms. I disliked it, as I did most of my suite at Whitehall, and indeed the entire palace, with its endless rooms and wings and courtyards and hallways. After two years, I still relied on my attendants to navigate them. But it was clear that his visit was related to the current crisis, and since James was not coming himself, he must have felt awkward speaking to me about it. Most likely, it would be about Anna's Catholicism, and so I wanted a setting that would remind Cecil that I was queen, and help me deflect any suspicion or criticism. Many of the Catholics at court had already been interrogated, but I was not going to allow that to happen to Anna. I'd spoken with her several days ago and believed her assurances that she remained as distant from religious politics as always.

I dressed in a satin gown of green and white, the colours of Queen Elizabeth, and wore an aigrette of emeralds in my hair. Cecil had served the late queen with devotion, and although I was a very different type of queen, I would expect nothing less than the same respect he had afforded her. His intellect and perceptiveness were legendary, and the significance of the colours would not be lost on him. I gathered most of my household into the reception room with me, not only my women but also my officers, ushers, secretaries, knights, musicians, and all of their servants. They stood in two long rows extending from my chair to the door. Everyone was to silently face the Secretary as he entered and came down the aisle to me.

But when Cecil arrived, he merely walked past the staring men and women as though he'd expected them. I realised that he must have been told they'd be so arranged, but it wouldn't have mattered if he hadn't. My attempt to intimidate him had been futile and foolish, as had my choice of a green and white velvet dress.

When, after he bowed, he asked me to dismiss everyone so we might speak alone, I meekly complied. As they left, he said distinctly, "Your Majesty, you compliment me with the colours of the last queen. It is a tribute to the many years I served her. The gesture is appreciated and taken as a token of friendship."

A whisper ran through the departing household members, many of whom looked back as though they would have liked to stay behind. But they did not, and soon the room was empty except for me and Cecil. He was a man who couldn't be judged from his appearance; except for his fine clothing, he easily could have been mistaken for a clerk. His body was frail and misshapen, his uneven shoulders only slightly concealed by his pleated white ruff and loose-sleeved black coat. He was middle-aged but looked older, his full head of smooth, light brown hair something of a surprise. It framed a long, pale face whose expression was always sadly thoughtful. But the way he held his hat with both his hands looked very determined, a departure from his otherwise gentle appearance.

In my chair my own stillness mirrored his. He had shifted the reason for my choice of dress, which he had certainly known, so as to begin in a more congenial manner. But I would not be so easily led. "Mr. Secretary, I was not aware you regarded me as a friend."

"We have had little reason for it, until now. But in friendship, I hope to serve you as well as I did Queen Elizabeth."

"Perhaps," I answered noncommittally. "But you have not come here today simply to state your friendship. You have a specific reason. I believe I know what it is. You have come to discover if my waiting woman Anna has been involved in these unfortunate recent matters."

"I already know she has not." His tone was polite but direct. "The king, myself, and certain members of our council, all know that although she is a Catholic, she avoids politics. It is also known by the Catholics. There were attempts to draw her towards them in your first months here, but she rejected them."

"I did the same when approached."

"That is also known to us. And we are aware that you are not a Catholic, as she is — despite your support for the Spanish marriage for your son."

"Which you, Mr. Secretary, did not support."

"The terms were unreasonable. In principle I do not oppose it. Neither does the king. It could have advantages and might possibly be returned to later. But that depends on many things, including the successful resolution of this new problem here in our own country."

Cecil was again trying to set me at ease, offering something I would find appealing. It did appeal to me, but I wasn't going to let him know it yet. "Anna is content to practise her own religion while remaining loyal to the king and following his policies."

"Our hopes have been for other Catholics to follow her example. Many have, but, as we have witnessed, not all." Weariness entered his voice, although his manner remained composed. "The majority of Catholics in this land do not want religion involved with politics. The few that do are often motivated by secular reasons that have nothing to do with religion, which becomes a convenient excuse. Some truly act out of belief, but even then, the religious cause often occupies a vacancy in their lives. So it has been for thirty-five years, since the Pope excommunicated Queen Elizabeth, and so it is with those who have plotted against us today."

I almost offered an objection, for I believed many Catholics were sincere in their religion. But I saw it would have no effect on him, for his life had been too entangled in political events. Besides, there was truth to what he said, and I had often thought as much about Anna.

Cecil went on, "Only one of the men involved with this new plot was knighted. The others were not, nor were they accomplished in any significant way. None of the nobility were directly involved, and it is doubtful even those with some weak ties to the participants were more than unknowing bystanders. It is one aspect of this sorry situation for which we should be grateful, for it shows the Catholic interest is now even less than thirty-five years ago. Back then, a handful of the northern lords supported the cause. But not now."

"So, no one else abetted this insurrection?" It was exactly what I had wanted to hear, that the plot had been small, involving only a few. Soon, then it would be behind us.

"We suspect the Jesuits. It would not be surprising, given their history of sowing discord here. For years the order has been secretly sending priests to our shores. More than any other Catholics they are committed to restoring their religion. It was they who were behind the plots to remove the last queen."

"Such things do the Catholics here no good." Finally, I trusted him enough to show I was in agreement.

"Indeed, they do not, Your Majesty. Quite the opposite; it makes it more difficult for those who are law-abiding and wish to live quietly. Also, for those who are our friends." He paused meaningfully. "In the past days there have been protests outside the residence of the Spanish ambassador."

For the next few moments neither of us spoke. "This is the reason for your visit today," I then said quietly. "You know I recently made a gift to him. And you must also know he responded with a statement of friendship." When I had first decided to make the gift, I had expected it would eventually become known to James, and others. I now repeated what I had told Mr. Heriot when ordering it: "The gift was given out of gratitude for his successful completion of the treaty."

As soon as I said it, I wished I hadn't, for it would be foolish to believe Cecil didn't understand my real intention had been to lay a path that might lead to a future Spanish marriage for Henry.

"Mr. Secretary," I said, "you have come here to suggest that friendship be ended."

"No, Your Majesty. We know he wasn't involved in the plot. The Spanish are as interested in harmony between our countries as we are. Although since we now touch on the matter, I would suggest that there be no further gifts to him for a while. As I said, there have been crowds protesting at his residence. But this is not my reason for visiting you today."

I felt I had entered a maze, certain of how to navigate it, only to find myself turned about and not knowing which path to take. "Then what is?"

"We have new information about the foiled plot. It concerns your family, differently from what was already known to us."

Immediately I knew I was about to hear something I didn't want to, and that would have serious consequences. In the past, James had always been the one to speak to me about anything important regarding either myself or the children. Never had he sent anyone else. "Why did the king not come himself, as he always does?"

There was a new touch of sympathy in Cecil's voice as he answered, "He did not tell me. When the king makes a request of me, it is not my place to question it. But I think, Your Majesty, that perhaps he was disturbed by the news in a personal way, as much as a kingly one." Since the start of our conversation, he hadn't moved, but now he did, shifting his weight from one leg to the other. "We have learned that after the —" he hesitated in his choice of word — "removal of the king and his sons, your daughter Elizabeth was to become queen."

At first what he said was incomprehensible. Then, suddenly, I understood the truth of his words. "Yes, that's what they would have done, wouldn't they? Installed a child they could manipulate," I said. "When she was old enough, they would have married her to some Catholic nobleman. She would never have been anything more than a puppet for her entire life." Cecil seemed to fade before me, replaced by an image of my daughter as the years passed, alone and friendless, a tool used by others.

Distantly, I heard him say, "Yes, they planned to rule through her." Elizabeth's image receded, and he was there again before me. He took a step closer to me. "Remember, Your Majesty, the danger is past. The plot was discovered in time."

But as I sat looking at him, I knew what he had just told me could cause a permanent change in my family. And, as he stood motionless before me, I saw that he knew it also. He was a man who had survived politically where others had not, and had done so through his wits. Likely long before we'd come to England, he'd known that James feared being replaced by his own child, as his mother had been by him. And he had also known that this could now easily provoke that fear in him again. It was especially difficult coming directly on the heels of the discovery of the planned use of gunpowder against him, as it had been against his father. A few days ago, James had sought me out to tell me, and I had helped him. But I might not be able to do so again. His having sent someone else with the news was not a good sign. And the gentle tone the secretary had taken had shown that he knew it..

Any doubts I had were erased when he said, "Your Majesty, it would be a service to all of England if you were able to help the king maintain his peace of mind during this difficult time. The country looks to him for harmony and stability."

He seemed to know better than to expect a reply from me. The conversation was over, his having done what he needed to, and he bowed and left. As he did, I vaguely wondered if he did indeed now regard me as a friend. My women started to come in after him, but I told them to wait outside. The Secretary's visit had been a distraction from the nausea, but now I noticed it again. In the silence of the empty reception room, I tried to reassure myself that when I saw James, I would find him the same as always. But I already knew I would not.

When I sought him an hour later, he was alone in his library. It was a favourite place of his at Whitehall, where he read, or wrote, or reviewed the work of the scholars on the new English translation of the Bible he was sponsoring. It was odd that he would be there during the day, but under the circumstances not unexpected. His anxieties had prompted a retreat to a place where he might calm them, but I didn't know whether I should take it as a good sign or not. I wished he'd come to me instead, as he had last time.

I entered his suite through the connecting passage to mine, accompanied only by Anna. The attendant gentlemen in the outer room stood in little clusters, whispering, and all turned in surprise as I entered, for I never visited James without sending a message first. All but one bowed and fell back to either side of the room out of the way as I passed through to the library door. The remaining one came to me, bowing, and said warningly, "Your Majesty, the king's dogs are with him. Perhaps we should inquire if he wishes them removed?" I shook my head. Although I hadn't known he had brought them from Royston, I was happy he'd done so, for when not hunting they always had a calming effect on him and could now be very useful.

I tried to smile at the guard by the door when I reached it, but I was sure it must have looked like a grimace. He knocked lightly, and a soft reply to enter was audible beyond the door. The guard opened it and announced me. Anna stepped back and I went in, the door creaking as it slowly shut.

James was standing by the window, leaning one arm against the frame as he looked out. Although his back was to me and his face not visible, there was a sad aspect to his posture, as though his greatest wish was to be anywhere else. "Anne," he said vaguely, without turning.

Several of the half dozen or so beagles, greyhounds and water spaniels came trotting over to me, their tails wagging. The sound of their paws on the stone floor caused him to turn around, revealing a young beagle, little more than a puppy, held close to him in his other arm. His face was blank and far from reassuring. He had a look of having already resolved his troubles, but if so, he had excluded me and our children from the process.

He came and sat down at the table in the centre of the room, holding the beagle on his lap. Then he snapped his fingers, and the other dogs that had been encircling me returned to him. I heard rather than saw them settle on the floor around him on the other side of the table. Without them, I felt alone. I wished he would ask me to sit, but he did not. Never before had he been so indifferent to me; even when we had been in the midst of a disagreement, he had remained polite.

I took a few steps towards him, then stopped. The table seemed like a barrier between us, piled with books and correspondence, and several Latin bibles. Yet if I tried to move around it, I would not be able to see his face, nor he mine, which seemed essential if what I had to say was to reach him at all. Uncertainly, I stood where I was, the words I had so carefully rehearsed now jumbling together.

Somehow, I found the ability to speak. "James," I began, tentatively, "the Secretary has visited me." Having managed to utter a few words, I felt more stable. There were several stools to one side of the desk for use of his clerks, and I pulled one over and sat down directly across from him. "He told me of the plot to make our daughter queen. It was despicable, and equally unsuccessful. But you must remember she was not a party to it, and would never have agreed to such a thing. None of our children ever would. It was an attempt to use her." I paused, then repeated, "She would never have agreed to it."

As I spoke, the invisible wall between us remained intact. One of his hands ran back and forth over the smooth coat of the beagle on his lap. Beside him, a greyhound pressed its head against his arm. I waited for him to comment, but he merely looked at me.

There was nothing for me to do but continue. "This can only have been a terrible shock for you. I understand it as few do. It reminds you of how your mother was replaced on the throne by you. Under any circumstances, this would be difficult for you — or for anyone it had happened to — to move past. Coming on the heels of the reminder of the tragedy of your father, whose attempted destruction by gunpowder was also mirrored by this plot, must make it unbearable. But these matters are not the same, neither in intent nor outcome."

Finally, he spoke. "It was why Queen Elizabeth never named a successor. She feared being replaced. It was why she never had a child. Now, I understand it."

I wanted to deny it, but we both knew it was true. "James, her situation was very different from yours. There was always the question of her legitimacy. The English people would never have such doubts about you. This plot would never have succeeded. And as I said before, our daughter would never have agreed to it."

"Were the rest of us dead, there would have been no other choice. Neither for her, nor the people of this land."

Again, I wanted to say something, but before any reply could form, he went on, "Such is the way of it when one in my position has children."

The invisible wall between us seemed unbreakable. But still, I said, "You have had a shock. It influences how you feel about this matter. Feelings change, over time."

"I acknowledge that God has blessed me with four children." He said it without emotion, as though it were a prayer recited so many times it had become meaningless. "And I am grateful." His eyes closed, and when they reopened I saw that something had changed within him. With a cheerfulness almost blatantly false, he said, "You make more of this than you need to, Anne. Please, do not be so troubled by it. I assure you, I am not."

His empty words were but another barrier to my reassuring him that nothing had changed within our family. But I saw that at present it would be useless for me to continue to try to remind him of it. I would have to try again later. Hopefully the outcome would be different from what it had been today.

It was then that I told him I was once again with child. His response was to stare at me emptily and continue stroking the beagle in his lap.

5

The trial of the conspirators took place in January. James insisted that Henry and I attend, although I would have preferred not to. My morning nausea had not only continued but had been worse than any I had experienced carrying my other children. Although it abated somewhat as the day progressed, it left me tired and uncomfortable, and not wanting to appear in public any more than I had to, least of all in a situation as stressful as a trial. I also did not relish entering the building where such a brutal demise had been planned for us, and neither did I wish for Henry to go there and hear the details of the plot. But James wanted him to be aware of the dangers that surrounded us.

I thought the three of us together in the same courtroom with those who had sought our destruction might somehow help James banish the personal fears the plot had provoked in him. The quiet and withdrawn mood that had come over him had remained constant ever since. Even the gradual revelation of the limited and circumscribed nature of the plot, without widespread English or foreign or papal support, had not drawn him out of it. When it had been reported to him that Elizabeth, upon being told of the plan for her to replace him, had replied she would rather have died with her family, he had barely responded. The Christmas and New Year celebrations, in stark contrast to the two earlier ones we'd had in England, had been nearly dismal. James had participated in the most obligatory manner, resisting attempts by myself, the children, and the courtiers to draw him further into the festivities.

Everyone knew the trial was merely for show, an important public display.. I was pleased to learn beforehand that there was a private room next to Westminster Hall with screened windows from which we could watch the proceedings without being seen. When we arrived, we found more than one such observation space had been prepared, and James's was separate from Henry's and mine. Although this was disappointing because of my desire for family unity, it allowed me to concentrate more on Henry. Two comfortable chairs had been set for us before the windows, with others for a select group of our attendants behind. As long as we spoke in low voices, we wouldn't be heard in the courtroom, where the earls serving as commissioners were already in their places at a long table.

Henry, who would turn twelve in a month, had remained at Whitehall in expectation of attending the trial after the holidays, while the other children had returned to their homes. It was difficult to tell if the plot had affected him. Each time I saw him, he seemed to keep more of his opinions to himself. But unlike many mostly silent people, he didn't seem so because he was observing those around him. Very few people appeared to interest him. Instead, he was absorbed by issues of society and government, and military and commercial matters. Although proficient at his studies, he was in no way a scholar like his father, but he had a similar dislike of frivolous court pastimes such as dancing, even though he was a much better dancer than James. He had absolutely none of the intellectual wit his father was able to utilise to make his way through awkward situations. The main interest the two shared was hunting. Rarely did Henry display emotions, but when he did, they appeared deep.

The trial, I knew, would interest him, and as we took our seats before the windows, his almost brooding demeanour for once told me exactly where his thoughts were. I asked, "Do you notice the absence of any feeling of mystery or expectation about this trial? I think it's unusual, is it not?" I gestured to the window. "The mood out there seems subdued, much the way it has felt in the palace. I suppose it's because the verdict is a foregone conclusion."

"They are going to be found guilty," he answered. "The trial is just for show."

"It is important as a deterrent."

"This can never happen again," he said flatly. "Never."

All conversation beyond the windows suddenly stopped, and looking out, we saw the prisoners being led in. There were eight of them, unkempt and dishevelled in appearance and attire, but their demeanours differed, with some looking distraught, others indifferent. But for the most part, all looked like average English gentlemen, not courtiers, but the type one saw around the fringes of the palaces. I stared at them, feeling a little confused for the first time since having learned of the plot. It was difficult to believe these ordinary and mostly mild-looking men could have intended such violence towards me and my family. When a few minutes later their names were read aloud in the indictment, they also sounded like those of typical Englishmen: Guy Fawkes, Thomas Wintour, Robert Wintour, Robert Keyes, Thomas Bates, John Grant, Everard Digby, Ambrose Rookwood. They could easily have been the names of the gentlemen of my household. The other names read out — those who had already died either trying to avoid capture, or later in prison, and the still uncaptured Jesuit priests — again sounded like typical Englishmen one could encounter anywhere in the country.

But interspersed among their names, the words 'traitor' and 'treason' were constantly repeated, a reminder that no matter how ordinary they looked, the men were far from being so. They had sought to destroy us, and I would not allow myself to think of them in any other way. I began to wonder how it would be possible to live in a world where traitors could be so disguised. My anxiety grew and I wanted to leave the little room where we sat, and the entire situation that had brought us there. I tried directing my thoughts elsewhere — to what gifts I would bring when I visited Mary in a month or so; to new gowns I wanted to have made; to possible names for the child I was carrying. But then, Henry moved slightly in his chair beside me, calling my attention back to the trial. A murmur was running through the crowd. I touched Henry's arm and asked, "What has happened?"

"They all responded 'not guilty' to the indictment," he said. "They claim their actions were for the country and directed by God." Quickly, he turned to look at me. "They are wrong. What they wanted to do was not for the country. And God had no part in it." He spoke with calmness and certainty. "They are guilty," he concluded. "The consequences are deserved." Looking back to the window, he added, "These Catholics are despicable."

"Henry, you usually do not have so much to say."

"At times it is important to speak the truth."

"But truth can be interpreted differently. Especially in matters of religion."

This time he did not reply, but his silence was pointed and told me plainly that he did not agree. I considered telling him it did no good to view religion so narrowly, since the world was filled with many who believed differently from us, and with whom one had to co-exist. But the setting was not appropriate, with courtiers behind us, listening to what we said. And the trial was resuming, and Henry's attention would be fixed on it.

The charges of the indictment were read: firstly, to deprive the king of his crown; secondly, to murder the king, the queen, and the prince; thirdly, to stir rebellion and sedition in the country; fourthly, to bring a miserable destruction among the subjects; fifthly, to change, alter and subvert the religion here established; and sixthly, to ruinate the state of the Commonwealth, and to bring in strangers to invade it.

Other statements followed, read out in the same dispassionate voice, declaring the conspirators' intention to destroy the king's entire male progeny, meaning Charles in addition to Henry, but to spare Elizabeth and Mary. Elizabeth would have been queen, but a very different one from the cousin she'd been named for, without a shred of the self-determination the late Elizabeth had been known for. The birthrights of both my daughters would have been stolen, used by the men who married them to validate their own authority.

Whatever slight sympathy I'd had for the conspirators as men misguided by beliefs not in accord with mine, whatever Christian duties I'd been taught of loving one's enemies, and of mercy and forgiveness, vanished in a way that I somehow knew was permanent. The men on trial had wanted either the outright destruction of those I loved most, or the manipulation of our legacy. From the beginning, I had known that all would be found guilty and judged accordingly. But thus far I had avoided acknowledging that the deaths to which they would certainly be sentenced were what I personally felt they deserved. Now, with perfect clarity, I knew it was what I wanted. It was a revelation to me that such feelings could exist within me. For the first time, certain truths about being a king or a queen were apparent to me, and I now understood that James had already been aware of them, and always had. During our life together, an imbalance had existed between us. As I sat staring at the little window before me, I could only wonder if my husband was truly such a stranger to me.

Beyond that window the river of words was continuing, flowing through its already set course towards its conclusion. Beside me Henry sat listening and watching, set upon following and comprehending every moment. But those words now seemed unintelligible and meaningless to me. I beckoned for Anna, whispering for her to go and inquire how long the rest of the trial was likely to take. When she returned and whispered that it would probably go on for the rest of the day, I knew it would be intolerable for me to remain. My condition would allow me to leave, and this time I sent Anna to James to ask if he would object to my departure. His reply came quickly: I could go, but Henry should stay and be brought to the little room where he was. I started to send another message back that I wanted Henry to accompany me, but I stopped. Henry would be king one day, and needed to understand what would be required of him.

6

I wrote to my brother shortly after the beginning of May:

The execution of the last of the conspirators took place yesterday. As you know, most were in January, but this one, a Catholic priest who has for years been a key figure in efforts to restore that religion here, had been in hiding and was only found later.

Now that this sorry business is behind us, the king and I hope the plans for your visit can be finalised. Of course, by necessity the official attitude towards Catholics here has become more stringent, and both James and Secretary Cecil feel a visit at this time of the King of Denmark, one of the most powerful and influential Reformed leaders of modern Europe, would make a clear statement of stability as well as the future direction of this country.

Of equal importance is that I am to be confined at the end of June, and your arrival during the summer would allow our new child the honour of having you as godparent. And, my dearest brother, it would give me great joy to see you again after so many years.

I signed my name beneath, then gave the letter to Anna for delivery to Secretary Cecil, who would enclose it within the state letter he was sending. It was just a formality, for the visit was in truth already agreed upon, but it had been felt that a personal note from me would add a touch of familiarity which might be important should Christian be having any second thoughts about the trip.

"Take this away also," I told Anna, sliding down towards my knees the little writing table that straddled my lap while I was in bed. By now I was so great with child that I'd almost been unable to draw it close enough to use effectively. She lifted it easily and took it away with the letter. Then, I motioned for my women to help me up. "I want to look out on the gardens."

Coming to Greenwich Palace had been a welcome change. All along my plans had been to go into seclusion here the usual several weeks before giving birth, as I had with Mary. But in direct contrast to that pregnancy, this one had been the most uncomfortable I'd yet experienced, with many sleepless hours at night as the child had moved incessantly within me, and food sensitivities and nausea that had continued for months longer than they had any time before. My feet and ankles had swelled, making walking uncomfortable. I could barely remember when I hadn't felt so irritable for most of the day.

At times I'd wondered if all the tension from the foiled plot had contributed to it, transitioning into my body and warning the child I was carrying of the difficult and dangerous world it would be entering. Our near-destruction had cast a pall not only over our family, but also over the court and the entire country. Worst of all, James hadn't fully shaken off the brooding melancholy that had taken hold of him. Most people wouldn't have noticed it, for his performance of his official duties was faultless, and he did seem to find steadiness and purpose in his work, which continued to interest him. He took efforts to engage with me and the children, but always there was a remoteness in his manner that had never been there before. The spontaneity and enthusiasm that had grown since coming to England was gone.

Very gently, some of the women folded back the smooth silk sheet and helped me slide my legs over the side of the bed. One brought a pair of slippers, which were pink velvet embroidered with pretty flowers. Because of my swollen feet, they were a much larger size than I usually wore, as though made for a giantess. It was fortunate that I was queen with so many attendants, for it would have been impossible for me to reach down to do it myself.

"A chair before the windows, please," I said. A nearby chair was pulled into position, and cushions were brought for the seat and back. Slowly, so the discomfort from my feet and ankles might not cause a stumble and fall, I walked around the room a bit, a woman on each side of me, holding my arms. When I'd had enough, I told them to take me to the chair. I settled into it, the footstool that was brought to raise my feet providing some relief from the pressure and making me more comfortable.

The windows were open, and I could feel the slight May breeze and see the swaying of the pale green foliage. The decision to come here earlier than needed had been a good one. Traces of the joy and promise of Mary's birth here a year ago seemed to be lingering about. It had been a crowning moment in the success we'd enjoyed throughout our first two years in England, before everything had been tarnished by the gunpowder plot and its dreadful consequences.

After a few minutes I asked for the Countess of Bedford to be sent for, when I finally felt easy enough not to complain of my physical discomfort to her. She was childless, and so speaking to her of such things would be insensitive. But I would tell her my other concerns, for she was always able to reassure me as few others could. I was already waiting for her report from her overnight trip to Mary's household in Stanwell, where I'd sent her to assess the princess's progress and welfare, my own monthly visits having been curtailed some time ago because of my increasing discomfort. She had returned around midday, and I'd allowed her time to rest from the trip before coming to me.

"The princess flourishes!" she announced behind me as she came in, before she swept into view between me and the windows. She still wore her stylish dark red travelling outfit, which made it clear that she hadn't been resting. Her cultural activities beyond her formal court duties were endless, especially her patronage of writers and artists, and a day's absence from London would have presented her with a myriad of matters to attend to on her return. But even so, she still looked fresh and enthusiastic as she curtsied.

"Sit." I pointed to the window seat behind her, which she backed towards, expertly flicking the skirt of her satin dress to one side as she sank onto it. "My daughter is well?"

"Extremely. She not only walks, but runs, though she still totters a little. I saw for myself. By the time she's brought here for the new child's christening, she should be steady. She is also quite beautiful, with promise of resemblance to her sister. But most of all, she enjoys good health and grows appropriately. Your Majesty can rest easily, knowing that she is in good hands."

"I am grateful to you for having visited."

"It was an honour." She peered at my face and then down at my feet. "The swelling is still no better?" The concern in her voice was genuine.

"Not any worse, at least."

Her brown eyes, always intelligent, fixed on my face searchingly. "Then what is it that troubles you?"

I raised my hand and gave a little wave backwards over my shoulder, signalling that I wanted everyone else to leave. From various places throughout the bedroom, I heard the sweep of dresses as all the women went out.

"Gone," said the countess as I heard the door close. At once, I burst into tears, which had come on so suddenly they surprised even me.

Without saying a word, she reached into a pocket and produced a lace-trimmed handkerchief, its perfect whiteness and delicacy contrasting with her sleek and bold attire. Her gentleness also seemed at odds with her alert and briskly competent manner. "Unused," she said, with a touch of humour, as she brought the handkerchief to me.

She returned to the window seat and waited while I wiped my eyes. "It's being here at Greenwich," I said. "I'm glad I came. But I also remember how different it was when Mary was born. How could things have so changed in a year?"

"Such is life. You know that. And you also know more changes follow, always, and things can reverse themselves. I'd say they've already begun to do so, with the conclusion of these executions. I think the birth of this new child might be the perfect restorative."

"Perhaps," I said hopefully, but without commitment. "Although in some ways I've felt that my being with child these past months has been unfortunate timing. With James, it's been an obstacle to our intimacy. What happens when he comes to my bed has always been a powerful bond between us, away from the complexities and artificiality of being king and queen. But on my doctors' orders my condition has prevented it since the plot was discovered. Had he been in my bed these past months, he might have remembered we are husband and wife, and parents of children, even more than we are royalty. The melancholy still lingering in him might now be gone." I rested both my hands protectively over my midsection. "And now, I fear his attitude towards this new child might be the same."

"But even if so," the countess replied, softly but earnestly, "a month after you're delivered, he can return to your bed again. He won't have forgotten what passed there between you. And everything should turn right again."

"As usual, you reassure me."

"You've told me how your marriage survived political turmoil in Scotland."

"It did," I acknowledged. The struggle between James and me over how Henry was to be raised had been bitter. In the end, what had got us through it intact had been the core stability of our marriage, and our joint ambition to secure the English throne for our children. But in Scotland we'd had less ceremony and protocol in our daily lives distancing us from each other. And of course, now the English throne was ours. More than ever, the resumption of our bedroom intimacy was going to be important in bringing James back to being the loving father and husband he'd been before. Hopefully the countess's prediction that everything would turn right again would come true.

She reached back and pushed the window behind her even further open. The breeze increased, soothing me. My child moved within me.

The countess noticed the change in me and changed the direction of our conversation, telling me of the various writers and artists she was patronising. "And I have several architects and designers I want you to meet for Somerset House."

Somerset House, the grand mansion built more than half a century ago by the Lord Protector, had been given to me by Parliament for my London residence upon my becoming queen. Although at first hesitant, after seeing it I'd been taken by the opportunities to make the mansion into a work of art, renovating it as I pleased. I had immediately, assisted by the countess, begun to plan for the changes. But there had been delays over the following three years, first as I had learned and became accustomed to what was required of me as English queen, and the intricacies of the court and society, and overseeing the establishment of my children's households. Then, there had been the priority of all things relating to Mary's birth, followed by the same for the new child, and the distractions of the political unrest. Soon, though, I would be able to start to implement the ideas I'd had for the mansion — even though for most of the upcoming months I'd be needing to spend more time in residence with James, wherever he was.

For the next hour, the countess told me of work that had been done on palaces and mansions on the continent, and the new styles. So vivid were her descriptions that I became thoroughly caught up in envisioning the outcome for Denmark House, completely distracted from my bodily discomfort and anxieties. By the time she left, I was so improved that I decided to have my women dress me to go downstairs for supper with my court and household in the banquet hall.

Doing so was ambitious, for although everyone knew I was with child, when I was in public it was still important to present myself as a queen with no imperfections. In Scotland, it hadn't mattered, but the English standards for how we appeared were as structured and formal as all the other protocols for us. Carefully and patiently, the Countess of Bedford and my other friends and senior attendants had upon my arrival made it known to me that since the English people were wealthier than the Scots, large sections of the populace had more time to think beyond the basic necessities of life, and to notice things and reflect upon them. What people saw, especially the commoners, was what they would remember, so James and I must never look weak or vulnerable. While expecting Mary I'd learned to make use of wider farthingales, cleverly designed to conceal my expanding midsection, and I knew which foods I could eat so as not to be taken with nausea when I dined in public. But even so, my miscarriages in Scotland, especially the late one, had been devastating, and I would still take the precaution of being carried downstairs in a chair, no matter who saw it. I wondered how many women had to contend with similar discomfort for the world to continue, but with none of the luxuries I enjoyed.

Two weeks later, Christian responded that he looked forward to his visit with eagerness and would arrive as expected. Plans continued to be made for the visit, including a spectacular tournament to he held here at Greenwich.

At the beginning of June, shortly after I entered my seclusion, Anna told me, "A challenge has been issued for the tournament, in the name of Four Knights Errant of the Fortunate Island. It's said that when the king read it, he found it so funny he laughed aloud." She then looked at me knowingly and said, "The king's dark mood improves."

It was the first report I'd heard in months of his showing any mirth. Perhaps our time of troubles was indeed about to be left behind. "Pray it continues to do so," I replied, not caring that her prayers would be Catholic. Added to my own Anglican ones, they might only help. All of us, Catholic and Anglican alike, could only feel easier if James's mind became free of fear and suspicion, and things became stable again.

7

During the final weeks of my pregnancy, the same discomforts continued, but I tolerated them, knowing they would shortly be over. It was a relief when before dawn on the date predicted, the familiar flow of water came and the contractions began. The doctors and midwives were called. James, who was already at Greenwich with his courtiers, was informed immediately, and went to the chapel to pray for a safe delivery. The main doctor, known for his expertise in delivery, examined me and said that although my labour might not be as quick as with Mary — slightly more than three hours — he did not expect more than half a day, with the child taking its first breath around noon. The midwives brought the birthing stool and the various linens, ointments and herbs that might be needed.

By noon, the child had not arrived, the contractions having settled into a slow pattern without progression. I was assured by all that though it was disappointing, it was normal for women to take up to twelve hours to deliver. From my own experience, I knew it to be true. Soon, the contractions would increase in frequency, and I would be able to go to the birthing stool to encourage the child's emergence, which would not be long after. But by dusk, there had been no change, except that I was becoming tired. Only with effort was I able to walk about the room, assisted by my women, hoping the motion might encourage the birth.

"What more can be done?" I asked the doctor. He conferred hurriedly with the midwives, who then brought me to the bed and expertly began gently pressing and rubbing my body in various places, especially around my lower back, while crushed herbs were held against my nose for me to inhale. The manipulation relieved some of the pressure, and I felt stronger, better able to withstand the contractions, but by midnight they had still not increased. I was becoming weaker again, not even sure I could leave my bed for the birthing stool.

James had long since left the chapel, and throughout the day sent various messages of love and encouragement to me, through Anna. In the evening, he had come to my suite and remained in the outer room, a show of support I was able to appreciate despite my frustration and distress. I was becoming hazy about the passage of time, but as best I could tell, about an hour after midnight, one of the doctors approached and bent to speak to me. "We have just conferred with the king, Your Majesty," he said calmly but urgently. "I am skilled with the use of an instrument that has been used with great success in cases such as yours. It helps save both mother and child."

"Is it so desperate?" I was barely able to ask the question.

"Not yet, but we are approaching when it can become so. You haven't lost blood. But if we wait longer with no change, it can be dangerous. The instrument is most successful when used while the mother still has strength."

I was clear enough to ask, "What instrument? I've never heard of such a thing."

"It has been kept secret for use only for the royalty or nobility of Europe. The instrument is a pair of forceps. We gently reach within and assist the child's emergence by pulling. The king has already given us permission."

I could not even reply. For James to have agreed meant my life and the child's were already in danger. It would be useless for me to resist, even if I wanted to.

The doctor stepped away from the bed. An instant later, Anna's face appeared where his had been. "Your Majesty!" she said with alarm. "News of Prince Henry! He is in great peril!"

Something within me jolted in fear, causing me to half rise from the pillow. "Henry! In peril?" Suddenly intensely awake and aware, a surge of dread passed through me. "What has happened —" I started to ask, but was stopped by a strong contraction, more powerful than any before it. I gasped for breath as another followed, and another.

"The child comes!" I heard Anna cry out, as indeed I felt the movement within me that had been so delayed.

"No time for the stool," the doctor said as he rushed towards me with the midwives, barely in time to receive the infant, whose final moments of emergence had become as swift and easy as the preceding hours had been difficult and prolonged.

Anna said, "Quickly, the king and observers!" Then she leaned in, her face almost touching mine. "The prince is fine," she told me.. "It was a lie to assist you. The midwives said a sudden fright might help. It did." Beyond the foot of the bed, I became aware of people entering the room.

"A daughter," the doctor said, before the slap, and her first cry. At once there were cheers and applause, which somehow gave me strength to take her in my arms, as the midwives gently drew a cover over my lower parts. "Perfectly formed and healthy," the doctor announced. "None the worse for her delayed entrance." Then James was beside me, gently placing the side of his hand against my cheek.

"Another princess," he said softly, and if he felt any disappointment at not having another son, he didn't show it.

"Sophia," I remembered to say, the name I'd chosen for a girl. "I want that name for her."

Mary had been named for his mother, so I doubted he'd object to naming our new daughter after mine, although we hadn't discussed it. "Sophia," he said, understanding and agreeing. One of the women lifted her from me and wrapped a piece of linen around her, and then James took her and turned to the court. "Princess Sophia," he announced.

"God bless Princess Sophia!" someone called out, and it was repeated by everyone in the room.

"The queen must rest now," I heard James say. Leaning over me, he added, "Our other children sleep. They can greet their sister tomorrow. For now, you must rest."

Only when they'd left, and I'd seen Sophia safely in Anna's arms being taken to the nursery, was my relief replaced by fatigue. With effort I remained awake until the afterbirth had passed. Anna returned and told me Sophia had been swaddled and was asleep in her cradle.

"You frightened me," I said as my sore and aching body began to relax, prompted by the contents of a cup the doctor had held to my lips and I'd drank deeply from.

"May God forgive me for the lie. But once I heard talk of an instrument, I knew your life was already in danger. It was the knowledge of the midwives that saved you and the child. They said a fright could provide the needed push. I knew I had only one chance, so I chose what I was certain of."

Exhausted, I slept. When I woke, I could tell from the light at the window that it was already late in the day. Only when I shifted position did I feel how my entire body ached. Lifting my head made me aware of how weak I still was.

Seeing me awake, Anna and some of the women came to the bed. "The time?" I asked.

"Mid-afternoon," Anna answered. So well did I know her that I could tell without her saying it that something was wrong. The women with her kept their gazes averted from my face.

"The child? Sophia?" Fear was already touching me.

"She doesn't nurse. She is weaker. The doctors and the midwives are doing what they can."

"Bring her to me."

Without a word, she left to get her. I told the women to bring pillows, and with their help and momentous effort on my part I sat up. Although I didn't know if I could nurse her myself, I had to try. And even if not, the touch and feel of my body might in some way strengthen her.

She was swaddled in soft linen, her face as sweet and delicate as those of the angels shown in the books created by monks hundreds of years ago. I held her gently but firmly, whispering encouragement as I tried to coax her to nurse from me. Finally, I stopped trying, but held her as her breathing seemed to grow feebler. It was heartbreaking, but despite my weariness I was resolved not to give in to grief while holding her. Tension and fear may have surrounded her while she grew inside me, but in my arms, she would have nothing but love and devotion as her experience of life, even if it were cruelly short.

After a time, the wet nurse came and tried again, but without change. Then, James came in. Sitting on the bed beside me, his face and manner were as they had been in the halcyon days before the plot. "Dearest Anne," he said as he took my hand, holding it for a moment without speaking, before continuing, "Sophia may not be with us long. The doctors feel we should baptise her as soon as possible."

"Yes," I said. "I understand."

Still holding my hand, he turned away to the others in the room and said something. There was hurried activity, and more people came in, among them the dean of the Royal Chapel. I tried to calm myself but felt a single tear slide down my face. James noticed it, and with a finger wiped it away.

Within minutes, the ceremony was over. I wanted to hold Sophia again but could feel I hadn't the strength. "The doctor says she won't wake again," James told me. "Better for her to rest in her cradle until she passes." He then insisted I lie all the way back down again, staying and helping my women arrange the pillows and covers comfortably about me.

The light at the window was nearly completely faded, dusk having settled in, when James returned and told me she was gone. "She lived but a day," he said sombrely.

"Her name meant wisdom," I said. "But for whom?"

In the dim grey light, I could just make out his features enough to see that for once he had no answer.

"I'll tell the children now," he said instead. "I spoke with them earlier about this likelihood. All were stoic — even Charles, who has no memory of our losses of other children in Scotland." He paused, as though remembering. Then, abruptly, he said, "Nine times have we conceived. Henry, Elizabeth, Charles and Mary live. Margaret and Robert lived a little while. Two never breathed. Sophia has lived one day. And us? We live." He smoothed the cover about my shoulders. "I'll tell the children," he repeated, and left.

I motioned for my women, and told them to draw the curtains around the bed. In the darkness sleep came with merciful quickness.

In a tiny coffin Sophia lay in state in the chapel at Greenwich for three days before being taken in a black velvet-draped barge on the Thames to Westminster Abbey for burial, accompanied by most of the courtiers. Even had I been strong enough to attend, the protocols of my time of seclusion didn't permit me to leave my rooms for several more weeks.

The Countess of Bedford remained behind with me. After we were told the procession of barges had left Greenwich, I said to her, "The fears born of the conspiracy and its aftermath affected Sophia as she grew, as though absorbed by me and then her. It weakened her. I'll never believe it otherwise. Such troubles caused my two miscarriages in Scotland. It's almost a miracle she went to term and lived at all. But even her one day of life may have helped us. Finally, James is himself again, as he was before the conspiracy. He seems to remember who I and our children are to him. The night Sophia died, he even spoke to me of all that we've had. I'd had hope a new child might bring this about, but I never thought it could happen in so brief a time. In her one day of life, Sophia has performed a great service for us. I grieve her death but can celebrate her life."

"Wisdom, Your Majesty," the countess said consolingly.

But then I was overcome by a great feeling of loss and emptiness. No matter what she may have brought me, Sophia who for so many months had been a part of me was now gone. The sudden thought of the now unnecessary cradle standing empty in the closed nursery brought me to tears. "I'll always resent what those conspirators have done to my family!" I exclaimed bitterly. "But those who so oppressed the Catholics are just as much to blame, for provoking it."

"Families such as yours intertwine with the state," the countess said. "You must teach your children how to weather adversities like this, for there is no one else who can understand them. Even those close to you like me never can."

Neither James nor our children had gone to Westminster, James prevented by tradition and the children by my not wanting them overwhelmed by the occasion or the place. That afternoon when James visited, he told me that before Sophia's coffin was removed from the chapel, he'd brought the children there for a final goodbye and to pray for her soul. When they joined us a few minutes later, he mentioned it again, prompting Charles to ask why prayers had been needed, for surely in Sophia's short life she'd done nothing to require them.

"Prayers," Henry was quick to answer, "are needed by all of us."

"True, indeed," James replied. But the indifferent inflection in his voice told of an absence of conviction never before lacking when he'd spoken of religion.

"Reformed prayers," Henry added. "Anglican, and others. Those of the Catholics are as meaningless as their sacraments."

"Silly popery," Elizabeth said, giggling.

"What's popery?" asked Charles.

Henry's nose wrinkled with disgust. "What the Pope tells the Catholics to do. He's the man in charge of them. Only a man, although he thinks he's more than that."

"Enough talk of religion," James said. "Your mother doesn't want to hear that. You're here to comfort her after our loss, not cause her distress."

I was grateful not only for his words but for the way he'd changed. The terrible blow of Sophie's death had indeed helped him remember we were much more than potential rivals to replace him as he had his mother. His colourless response to the children's talk of the Catholics led me to think that the plot against us, although ostensibly deepening his position against them, might instead have lessened the prominence of religion in his life, especially the stricter type. He could not have failed to notice how the intended violence of the conspirators had circled back on them. Also, the gentler and more beauteous surroundings of England, less harsh and abrasive than Scotland, might have altered his view of life and what would follow it. If so, a grand Spanish marriage for Henry might still come about. I would, though, have to ensure the unpleasant and disdainful attitude Henry had expressed towards the Catholics just now became more reasonable. But for today, his father's milder response was enough.

Christian, despite Sophia's loss, came as planned the following month. James and a number of courtiers, including an interpreter — Christian spoke no English — went to meet the Danish fleet when it anchored off Gravesend, and accompanied him to my suite in Greenwich Palace, where I was still secluded.

Although I hadn't seen him since I'd left Denmark so many years ago, I still would have recognised him if he'd arrived unexpectedly. A little more than two years younger than me, the resemblance between us was pronounced, in face and colouring, although he was shorter. His manner as we first formally greeted each other, but then embraced, was affectionate while still regal. In his black silver-slashed clothes and his hat with its gold coronet, studded with precious gems, he looked every inch the successful king he'd been for years.

I sat back down again, and James and Christian sat side by side a few feet before me, their English and Danish courtiers clustered behind them. Immediately, in Danish, Christian offered condolences for my recent bereavement. I replied that of course he could sympathise, for out of his four children only two had so far survived. A few steps away, the interpreter quietly translated for James. But we must, I added, be thankful for the ones we'd been blessed with. Christian agreed, adding that we should also be grateful for our own continued health, and that of our spouses.

Upon hearing this translated, James smiled and said, "We are honoured to have you in England. Although the tournament we'd planned has out of respect to our departed child been cancelled, we have many other fine entertainments for you and your companions. You must, though, make do with me as sole host until your sister resumes her place in society, in two weeks." The interpreter hurriedly translated, and Christian thanked James for his hospitality. And, he said, he eagerly looked forward to meeting our children.

I told him tomorrow when James brought him to London he would meet Charles, whose household was there, and then Henry when they'd moved on to Hampton Court. Later in the visit Elizabeth would come from Coombe Abbey, although Mary, too young for a visit to be meaningful, would remain at Stanwell. Unlike the royal family in Denmark, I explained, each of our children had its own household.

The polite half smile on James's face didn't waver as he heard this translated, and there wasn't the slightest indication from Christian that he remembered the turmoil the arrangement had caused in our marriage following Henry's birth. Although I hadn't at the time written to him directly of it, all of Europe had known of the bitter struggle between James and me that had become entangled in Scottish politics. But by now it should have been clear to everyone that the animosity had long ago been overcome, and any lingering remnants left behind in Scotland. The birth of two more children here in England was proof that our marriage was not only intact but harmonious.

Eager to move away from unpleasant memories, I told Christian that not only our children but many of the nobility were eager to meet him, and extend English hospitality. Knowing of his particular interest in the arts, I mentioned he was to be entertained by Secretary Cecil at his estate Theobalds with a masque of Solomon and Sheba. Unfortunately, I said, I wouldn't be appearing in it as I had in so many others since coming to England, as my time of post-childbirth seclusion would not have ended. But I could not let him visit England and not sample the art form of which I was becoming the most noted patroness.

"King Solomon," Christian then said pointedly. In Danish, he added that Solomon was as wise a king as his brother-in-law King James. His Danish companions enthusiastically murmured their approval, some applauding, while the words were quickly spoken in English by the translator. There were little exclamations of pleased agreement from James's courtiers while his smile became more pronounced, although his hooded eyelids seemed to lower a bit further, as though to conceal how pleased he'd truly been by the compliment.

"It takes a wise man to recognise another," he then replied, the translation causing Christian and the other Danes to look equally pleased.

Christian then gestured to one of his gentlemen, who withdrew something from his sleeve and gave it to him. "A gift," Christian said in Danish as he stepped towards me, "for my beloved sister, England's queen." One of his hands unfolded to reveal an exquisitely made star-shaped brooch of diamonds, set in gold.

"Lovely," I said appreciatively as I took it.

James laughed in a low, gentle way. "The queen's liking of jewels is already legendary."

My collection had grown substantially since coming to England where I'd received so many gifts, but I never failed to enjoy receiving a new one. I gave Christian a generous look of gratitude as I thanked him. Apparently in Copenhagen there were jewellers whose craftmanship would rival that of Mr. Heriot's. Even so, I would be sure to tell James to bring Christian to his shop when they visited the Royal Exchange as part of his London tour.

But Christian wasn't finished distributing our gifts yet, and opened his other hand to show an identical piece. "For the king," he said, handing it to James. Turning to the group behind him, he said, "Like twin stars to guide in the nightly firmament." The Danish courtiers applauded at once, the English joining in as soon as they heard the translation.

James, surprised, thanked him. "Let the twin stars of England and Denmark be a guide for all our European neighbours for many years to come." He had always enjoyed displaying his wit in front of an audience, but I hadn't heard him do so in nearly a year. Once again, I thought with pleasure that he was his old self again. Christian's visit was wonderfully opportune, a breeze of fresh air to clear away the troubles and disappointments of the past year.

Nothing would have pleased me more than to have left seclusion right then and participated in the many planned events, but even if the time-honoured childbearing rituals and protocols hadn't prevented it, my physical condition would have. Although major loss of blood and permanent damage had been avoided, and Anna's quick thinking had prevented the need for the forceps, the prolonged delivery had left me exhausted, and sore in places I'd never felt before. Despite daily improvement, I knew I would need to rest for the next two weeks to be strong and comfortable enough for socialising.

8

"Future births are possible," one of the doctors told me frankly, after examining me shortly after Christian's arrival. "Your good recovery makes us even more confident of it." Two midwives, who had at my insistence accompanied them, said they agreed.

"Should the next delivery be as difficult?" I asked, with some concern.

"Not likely, although nothing is certain. No two women are the same regarding later pregnancies." With a wave of his hand, he sent the midwives out of hearing range. "And remember, Your Majesty, I and some of the other doctors here are skilled with the use of forceps. Although the instrument is not for general usage, I assure you that many women of the royal and noble families of Europe are alive today because of it. But there is no reason to assume you'd have need of it, or that the preceding term would be as uncomfortable as this one was for you." He paused, then asked, "If I may speak freely, Your Majesty?"

"Please do."

"The surrounding dangers and turmoil of the conspiracy and its aftermath were a difficult environment for a woman to be carrying a child through."

"I have thought so myself."

"Those days are behind us, Your Majesty. There is every reason to believe your next term would be as smooth and easy as it was for Princess Mary."

I had the midwives brought back and asked them the same. Their ways of viewing things, and their stores of knowledge, although similar to that of the doctors were not identical, and I valued their opinions nearly as much. When they agreed, I felt confident that James and I would indeed have another child, possibly more. It was with positive expectations for what lay ahead that I resigned myself to missing the festivities of most of Christian's visit, and resolved to be sufficiently strong to participate in the important final ones before he departed.

I most regretted missing the masque of Solomon and Sheba. After many days of reports of James's and Christian's hunting, hawking, tennis-playing, riding in magnificent processions, and attending feasts and banquets with all kinds of entertainments, I insisted the Countess of Bedford join the court at Theobalds to be able to provide a full description of the masque. I had enjoyed masques more than any other art since coming to England. Although we'd had them in Scotland, they'd been rare, their sumptuous and elaborate scenery and costumes expensive to plan and present. Temperamentally, English society was much more suited to them, and I delighted in both viewing and participating in them. There was something so pleasing about dressing up to depict important historical or mythological scenes, as though a painting had been brought to life, along with a recitation of accompanying verses. Masques were things of great beauty and sophistication, and I was proud that Christian would see how cultured the Stuart court was.

"The Secretary outdid himself!" the countess reported upon her return the morning after the presentation.. "But I saw he would, from the first moments of the kings' arrival. The road approaching Theobalds was strewn with artificial oak leaves with the word *Welcome* on them, written in gold. More of the same gracefully floated down on everyone at the entrance gate from a fascinating mechanical oak tree, while a song of welcome was sung in the background. Seeing all this at the very start, I knew the masque would be splendid."

"An impressive welcome," I said, "but not surprising." Secretary Cecil, newly created Earl of Salisbury by James because of his help uncovering the conspiracy, was exerting himself to make a demonstration of his loyalty and devotion to James and his brother-in-law. Most likely, the entire visit would be costing him a small fortune.

"After their arrival, there was a two-day interval of mostly hunting and banquets," the countess continued. "Which I must say I found tedious. But my patience was amply rewarded by the masque. After the banquet, curtains were drawn back at the end of the large hall, revealing a scene of a gorgeously attired Solomon standing before his temple, somehow appearing to be of gleaming white marble and extending above and beyond the walls and ceiling of the hall. Solomon was flanked by his court, and the priests of the temple, and the common folk, all colourfully costumed, at least a hundred figures packed in around him. Trumpets sounded, and then, to a musical accompaniment, a beautifully gowned Queen of Sheba entered, ahead of a full procession. She went to Solomon and bowed low, had her servants present him with gifts, then turned and went to King James and King Christian, and gave them gifts too. She then returned to Solomon and stood at his side while richly costumed figures of Hope, Faith and Charity entered and gave Solomon more gifts. And finally, Victory and Peace came in, side by side. All in all, a spectacular masque! The music and recitations were well done, but it was the sight of it that was most impressive. The Secretary had understood that with the Danish king speaking no English, it would be better to emphasise the visuals."

I sighed, sorry to have missed it. But the goal of showing Christian a formidable example of our arts had been achieved. "And how did the two kings respond?" I asked.

"With great appreciation, Your Majesty," she answered without hesitation. "They, and everyone else there, thoroughly enjoyed themselves."

But a few days later, right after James and Christian had arrived back at Greenwich and before I'd seen either, I learned the masque had gone quite differently from what the countess had told me.

There was a small sitting room off my bedroom which I seldom used, but because of my seclusion from time to time I went into for a change of scenery. As in the bedroom, its window overlooked the palace gardens, but from the outside it wasn't as readily identifiable as part of my suite. Therefore, the courtiers did not maintain a deferential distance from the window, and if it was open, I could hear them talking or laughing beneath it. It amused me to listen to what was usually silly court gossip, and today, when I heard voices there, I motioned for the two women who'd accompanied me to go back to the bedroom, while I went closer to listen. Standing so I couldn't be seen, I looked down to see a gentleman from my household talking to a knight from James's, newly returned with him that day from Theobalds.

"Quite a sight, my friend, quite a sight!" the knight was gleefully saying.

"Both kings fully drunk?" The gentleman's voice was full of rapt interest.

"Everyone was drunk, even the masquers. The entire masque was a complete fiasco!" He laughed unkindly. "The Queen of Sheba must have been drunk too. When she brought her gifts of delicacies to King Christian, she stumbled forward right into him! Splat! The wine and cream and jellies and cakes went flying into his face and down his clothes, and she collapsed onto the floor before him. Everyone in the hall burst into laughter, none more hilariously than the two kings! Servants came running with napkins to clean King Christian, who, laughing like a madman, jumped up and helped Sheba to her feet, saying he'd dance with her. But after trying to bow he instead fell at her feet, too drunk to stand up again, and had to be carried away. As they took him past me, I could still see some of Sheba's gifts stuck to his beard and clothes."

"What did King James do?" the gentleman asked, through his own laughter.

"He was already slumped low in his chair, so full of wine was he. But he raised his goblet in a toast to King Solomon and ordered the masque to continue. The woman playing Hope appeared and tried to speak her part, but was so drunk she couldn't, and begged His Majesty to excuse her. Faith staggered after her, not even attempting hers. Charity at least was able to speak, and approached the king with gifts like Sheba's, but the laughter and shouts in the hall were so loud, expecting a repetition of the mishap with King Christian, they drowned out her words. She gave up and joined Hope and Faith, both vomiting beside Solomon. Victory and Peace then made a grand entrance, but some squabble arose between them, which those around them joined in with, resulting in a full brawl. Lord Salisbury had to come in with his servants and have them all thrown out. By then, the king had passed out from drunkenness, and he was carried out in his chair."

"Unbelievable!" said the gentleman, laughing.

"At least our king escaped being covered with food and drink," the knight said mirthfully.

"They all had a good time, for sure! Though not how they expected."

There was more laughter from both of them, which faded as they walked away. I waited a moment, then reached out and drew the window closed, as though doing so might prevent disappointing news from entering. But it was too late; I'd already heard it.

The stunned feeling that had come over me was now replaced by one of deflation. The fine art of which I was the leading patroness in England and that I'd been so proud for my brother to see had been a ridiculous travesty instead. Somehow it felt as though I myself had been ridiculed, as much an object of scornful laughter as the Queen of Sheba sprawled out on the floor before Christian and James.

Someone came in behind me, and I turned to find Anna. "Your Majesty," she said with concern, "is something wrong? You look disturbed."

Suddenly I was angry, especially with the countess for having deceived me. I would immediately confront her for doing so, and tell her my trust had been violated and I could never confide in her again. I started to tell Anna to send for her, but stopped. There was a possibility the knight had made the story up or exaggerated. Although I knew that both James and Christian drank, I'd never seen James do so excessively, and it was almost unbelievable that both would have done so to the point of stupor. Without even considering the poor example it would set, there would be the terrible insult to the Secretary, who had gone to such lengths and expense to provide a fitting entertainment.

"Anna, have you heard any gossip of how the visit to Theobalds went?" She had always been my most reliable source for whatever stories were circulating among the household staff, who knew her to listen much but repeat little. "Have those who've been with the kings at Theobalds returned with any stories — of drunkenness especially?"

She looked startled by the question, but barely paused before answering. "They talked of it as soon as they got back here today." She said it directly, with no tone of apology or sympathy, understanding that for her to do so would make it more difficult for me to hear.

"What did they say?"

"The kings were drunk for the entire visit. All their courtiers too, English and Danish both. Not just at Theobalds, but since they left here after the King of Denmark arrived."

There was no criticism in the way she'd said it; it was merely a simple statement of fact. I knew at once that the knight's description of the debacle of the masque had been accurate. There was no reason for me to subject myself to hearing it all again from Anna.

"Thank you," I replied, in a tone indicating I had no further questions.

Upon occasion, when we were alone, Anna still took the liberty of offering an unrequested opinion, which I never reproached her for. "Ignore it," she now said. "There has been no harm done by such raucous and unseemly behaviour. Everyone understands that if you had been present, things would have been quite different. For King James and the English, the rowdiness and carousing are understandable after such a dreadful year. And for King Christian and the Danes, the trip is an escape from the need to maintain dignified roles for the Danish. But you can ignore it — no one is going to tell you of it. I'm surprised you know about what happened."

"I overheard a conversation I wasn't meant to."

"Then do as I say. There'll be no repetition of that behaviour now that they're back at Greenwich. And in a few days, you'll be participating in everything again."

Her advice was good. I would follow it, not mentioning the masque to anyone, and redirecting any conversation that approached it. Neither would I confront the countess about her deception, for she had only been trying to protect me.

It was unfortunate the masque had turned out so, but in the end, it was of no consequence. I'd always suspected that James, although acting politely appreciative, had little interest in them, and I now saw that Christian likely hadn't either. In the future I would be more careful about assuming my tastes would be shared by others, who wouldn't want to offend me with disinterest. I would put the masque at Theobalds behind me, as though it had never happened.

Anna's prediction proved correct, and during their first visit to me after returning, neither James nor Christian spoke of the masque, other than James's remarking in passing that they had enjoyed the new Earl of Salisbury's hospitality. Recognising the title even before the interpreter translated, Christian said he wished he had so reliable and devoted a Secretary of State in Denmark. In Danish I replied that we had Mr Secretary's wisdom and prudence to thank for having eased the path for James to the English throne. Then I turned to James and repeated it in English.

"Very true," James agreed. "Despite my claim being the strongest, King Henry had feared us Scots and barred us from the succession. And the English have always had some distrust of foreigners." He laughed, gently but patronisingly. "No ways are as good as English ways, for many of them. Because England's an island, the English see themselves as different from other Europeans."

After the interpreter translated, Christian touched his forehead thoughtfully and asked were it not the same in Scotland, being part of that island too? This time, I translated Christian's question. Doing so made me feel more included in the easy familiarity that had developed between them.

"Scotland is much smaller," James answered, "and centuries ago found that to protect itself from its larger and stronger island neighbour, alliances with other countries were necessary — France, and of course Denmark. The Scots learned to appreciate foreigners in ways the English never had to."

"And so, our marriage," I said playfully, then repeated it in Danish to make sure the translator didn't lose the tone. Almost together, James and Christian voiced their agreement.

James, echoed in Danish by the interpreter, continued, "Robert Cecil was Secretary of State for Queen Elizabeth, and understood I would be the best to follow her. He estimated, correctly, that the resistance to a foreigner could be overcome by other advantages that would appeal to this country. I came not only with years of experience of being a king, but with a wife and three children. After so many years of an unmarried and childless queen, the English were ready for a change. Cecil was right. We made quite an impression when we arrived and were welcomed."

Christian said it must have helped that we'd named our children Henry and Elizabeth, the most notable of the Tudor sovereigns.

Hearing it in English, James said, "And Charles, for my father's brother. A reminder that I was Tudor on both my parents' sides, and that my father, another Henry, was English."

Christian then said his meetings with our children had been the finest times of his trip, exceeded only by his seeing me again, and, most of all, the times he'd spent with King James. For the king, he said, was still most important, and came before all. As his words were translated, he bowed to James, who was clearly flattered, and then to me. His gaze met mine, and I saw the shrewd intelligence beneath his charming and genial manner.

He in turn saw that I'd noticed, and unseen by anyone else in the room, winked at me. It was all I could do to prevent myself from smiling. Right then I knew he understood much about us, and how our family had been affected by the insecurities in James that had been caused by the conspiracy. It was suddenly clear that his trip had been partly motivated by brotherly concern for my wellbeing, both personal and political. I would need to find the time to have an extended conversation with him, just the two of us. It would have to be done casually, without giving James cause for suspicion that he'd been intentionally excluded.

That opportunity didn't arise easily. James thoroughly enjoyed Christian's company and was with him for much of the time. Christian became involved in the planning of a magnificent feast he was to host for me on the Danish ships before his departure, and I was still limited to my rooms. It wasn't until James was unexpectedly needed for several hours at Westminster a few days before the end of the visit that Christian and I were able to talk.

My seclusion finally being over, we took advantage of the mild summer day to walk in the palace gardens. They were in full bloom, with riots of colour everywhere, more vivid because the day, although without rain, was overcast. Even though except for Anna my gentlewomen spoke no Danish, we couldn't very well keep Christian's attendants beyond hearing distance without doing the same for mine. As soon as I waved them away, he at once did the same for his.

He extended an arm, which I rested my hand on, and we started down a path. Oddly, we had both dressed in the same colour, he in a yellow satin doublet and breeches, a grey gathered ruff at his neck, me in a pale yellow silk gown patterned with tiny flowers of a darker yellow, the ruff open and framing my face, the waist farthingale not as wide as I wore for formal occasions. Neither of us wore a hat, with the jewels we sometimes used in suggestion of our crowns. Although my hair had been styled back and up as usual, stray wispy curls had become unfixed and from time to time fluttered in the breeze, as did locks of his own blond hair. From a distance it might have looked like two strange large birds of the same type had landed in the gardens. Our similarity, and shared identity, was reassuring and made me feel supported in ways I often did not.

Although we'd finally found the privacy needed for our talk, we would have to keep it short enough to avoid causing comment that could reach James's ears. At once, I asked Christian if he'd come to see how we'd weathered the storm of the conspiracy.

He replied that I was perceptive. Although there'd been other reasons, he said, it had been the main one, and largely at the request of our mother. She'd remembered gunpowder had been used to murder James's father, and that after Henry's birth James had separated him from me, fearful of his being used to replace him. She'd worried that the conspiracy might have revived old fears for him, and she'd wanted Christian to visit to smooth any differences between us, had they recurred. He was quite the diplomat, he said, briefly turning to face me. He smiled and winked again in his charming way. Our mother had also felt that Christian's visit would enhance my status, reminding the English — and James — of my connection to one of the most powerful royal families in Europe.

I told him that indeed there had been a problem when James had withdrawn within himself, especially after learning of the conspirators' plans to kill us and make our daughter queen. But strangely, it had been the death of our daughter Sophia that had brought us together again.

He replied that our mother would be satisfied with his report that all was well between us.

I asked, with a little laugh, if he hadn't found it so, would he have whisked me away back to Denmark? He replied, laughing also, that he would have — and he would have brought all four of my children along, keeping us until King James and the English learned to better value the scions of the royal house of Denmark, the descendants of so many kings. When I then remarked that it would have been complicated to sweep the five of us unto his ships and away, he answered that such was his ability, he would have done so easily. And although I knew we were joking, something in his voice made sure that he could.

We walked a bit further, into a path flanked by red and white rose bushes. Feeling that our precious time alone shouldn't be wasted with silence, I said the first thing that came into my head — that I knew our mother only from our letters, as I had him, until this much-appreciated visit. I sighed and added that I supposed it would be the way of it with myself and my daughters, who undoubtedly would marry foreign rulers.

"I wanted to speak with you of the prince," he then said, in Danish, which we continued in.

"Henry?" I asked.

"Yes, Henry," he answered. "He's a fine young man, with a strong intellect and wide interests — everything one could expect and hope for in a prince. I hope that my son will be the same. But remember, Henry is Scottish — and so is his father, and the English dislike foreigners. When the time comes for their next king, the English might hold it against him. Especially if another candidate is available, who is English." He paused. "You already have one child who is."

I stopped walking and faced him directly. "Mary?" I asked, still more surprised than anxious over what he'd just said.

"She might be viewed as more suitable by the English, since she was born here. But I think not," he said quickly. "I think Henry will still be preferred, vastly so, for being male. But if in the future there is another son, one that would be English, he might be wanted instead. Henry might follow James as King of Scotland, but not England."

"A dreadful thought," I said.

"We need to continue walking," he told me. "You look perturbed, and the courtiers are still close enough to think something is wrong." We did, and the red and white rose bushes that flanked us now seemed like a serious warning, each the colour of the differing sides in the wars of Lancaster and York, arisen because a distant English king had had too many sons, whose descendants had vied for the throne.

"I am sorry to have disturbed you so," said Christian. "I am not entirely sure of English law regarding the matter. Also, James has told me that he wishes for the two kingdoms to be merged into one, Great Britian, which would eliminate any problem for young Henry succeeding. But James has also said there is opposition to the plan — again, due to England's fear of foreigners — and it might be difficult to bring the plan about."

"Henry has already been made Prince of Wales, which shows the English want him as James's successor," I replied defensively.

"But public opinion could change during the many long remaining years of James's reign," Christian pointed out. More gently, he added, "I've spoken of the matter because your attachment to Henry as your favourite is so obvious. But no matter how you plan for the future, one never knows what it might bring — even for those of us with great resources at our disposal. Perhaps it would be worthwhile to check with an expert about whether my understanding of the English succession laws is correct."

Light rain began to fall, and we turned to go back. I decided I would speak with the Secretary about what Christian had said. He would have good judgement about how the country's mood might be expected to shift in the years ahead.

When James returned from Westminster that night and we all supped together, I couldn't help but wonder whether he was already aware of the possible issues we may face regarding Henry's succession. Perhaps it didn't matter to him which child succeeded, so long as none threatened his throne while he was alive. And in the morning when Henry arrived from Hampton Court, already at nearly age thirteen looking like a young king among his own group of courtiers, I could think of nothing else. For him to be cheated out of the English throne would be intolerable.

Fortunately, the activity of the next day was distracting, causing my anxiety to somewhat recede. We travelled down the Thames and over to Chatham on the River Medway, where we boarded an English ship, completely hung with cloth of gold, for a banquet in a pavilion on its deck. Afterward we returned to shore and took coaches to a place affording a view of the entire navy, where we watched the naval canon salutes. The spectacle was magnificent, a display for Christian and the Danes of the extent of English maritime power. Henry watched the salute with rapt attention, and I was sure he was thinking of the day when it would be under his command. It seemed impossible for me to even consider his being disappointed of it.

We spent the night at Upnor Castle, a fortress built to protect the dockyards and ships of the royal navy by Queen Elizabeth, who had wisely foreseen at the start of her reign that eventually the Spanish fleet would arrive with a force to invade England. It had been her awareness of that possibility and actions so many years in advance that had prevented it. In the same way, I would be wise to learn if there was indeed any threat to Henry's succession, and if so, do what I could to prevent it.

The next day we joined the seven Danish ships anchored off Gravesend, where Christian had prepared a banquet in my honour. The ships, under the Danish flag, were intended to represent for me a visit to my native land. The deck of the largest, the prize of the Danish fleet, had been hung with arras and expensively decorated, and there Christian presented us with a feast rivalling any he'd enjoyed in England. During it, we all proclaimed pledges of eternal friendship between England and Denmark, each one accompanied by drums and trumpets and the firing of cannons on all the Danish ships. Afterward, Christian gave us farewell gifts in gratitude for our hospitality — for me, a portrait of himself in a magnificent frame, and for James, a jewel-encrusted sword and hanger. Then he pointed to the best of the Danish ships beside us, a warship, and made a gift of it to Henry. Nothing could have pleased me more, for it was a statement by a king of emerging authority, an acknowledgement that Henry would one day wear the English crown.

The concluding firework display was spectacular despite being in midafternoon so the Thames tide could carry us back that day. During it, the slender and uneven figure of the Secretary appeared nearby, clad in his usual sober black. He was conveniently alone, and when I approached him, everyone else was watching the fireworks and didn't notice.

"Your Majesty," he said as he bowed. Then he gestured upward as a particularly loud firework exploded. "An impressive display."

"Indeed."

He held out a hand; over his glove he wore a large diamond ring, unexpected and incongruous against his restrained clothing. "Your royal brother knows how to make other impressive displays as well. This was his parting gift to me."

"He told the king and I that he wishes he had a counsellor like you in Denmark. We replied that your value to us is beyond calculation. The Earldom of Salisbury was barely sufficient to show it."

He bowed again, showing his gratitude. He must have been wondering what I wanted, but his face remained composed. Although since the time of the conspiracy's discovery we'd known we could regard each other as allies, we'd kept a distance from each other.

James and I were to go to Windsor Castle for the rest of the summer, so I asked, "Can you come to Windsor one day next week? I'd prefer you to come at a time when the king is hunting. There is something I need to consult you about." I looked at him meaningfully. "We should say the visit is about extensive changes I wish to make at Somerset House, and I need advice about those you made at Theobalds." I dropped my voice to barely a whisper. "But of course, the matter is much more important. As always, I rely on your discretion."

Another firework exploded, and we both looked up as dazzling sparks of green and gold filled the sky, to the delighted exclamations and applause of everyone on deck.

"I'll find the appropriate time, Your Majesty," he said quietly, and without expression. But I knew he'd understood the importance of my request, and already I felt relieved. Although I seldom extended my hand for anyone to kiss, I now did. With equal quickness, he bent and touched his lips to my fingers. I then returned to my women, all staring upward in anticipation of the next display.

Christian and I both wept when we parted, and I wondered if I would ever see him again. As our ships went in different directions, I couldn't help feeling something had permanently changed in my life during the visit.

James had drunk freely of the excellent wine at the banquet and was soon dozing in his chair on deck. I left mine to join Henry, who'd remained at the stern, his gaze fixed on the ship Christian had given him, now following us up the Thames to Woolwich, where it would be fitted with his insignia. Three or four of his young companions stood near him, talking among themselves but not to him, as though not wanting to intrude on his solitary thoughts. They saw me approaching and all bowed as I reached them. Although Henry stood only a short distance away, his attention remained on his new ship.

"My son appreciates his gift," I said, trying to set an informal tone.

"The king of Denmark was astute in his choice, Your Majesty," one of Henry's companions replied.

"It holds his attention now, to the exclusion of his friends, it seems. And me."

Another companion stepped backward, and the others followed suit to alert Henry to my presence, but I gestured for them not to. "Leave him to his own thoughts," I said, smiling fondly.

All of their smiles mirrored mine before the one who'd already spoken answered, "The prince is often so. We know not to disturb him when he is."

"Does he imagine sea journeys to far-off lands like America, I wonder? He often spoke of hoping to do so, when he was younger."

"He used to, but no longer, Your Majesty."

So Henry had put away an impossible childhood dream. Impulsively, I asked, "What does he speak of now?"

The young man's reply was quick but measured, for he had already learned to be a courtier and had to be careful of possibly displeasing Henry by saying too much. "The finance of such journeys, instead, and broad plans of their benefit to England."

"And what else?"

"All things, Your Majesty. Art, politics, and our studies. But he says nothing without carefully considering his words first. And it is almost impossible to tell what he is thinking."

I looked around at the others, asking, "Do you all agree?"

Immediately, all said they did.

"Thank you, young gentlemen, for your companionship to my son," I said. "I think now I'll follow your example of not disturbing his thoughts."

Their youth still allowed them enough spontaneity to show they liked my response, and all smiled as they bowed. I turned away to go back to my chair beside James's. If Henry had been reminded by his new ship of his now abandoned hopes of maritime exploration, I would not deprive him of his fantasies, for surely they would be fleeting. More likely he was now imagining himself in his future role with the entire English fleet under his command. Once again, as I sat back down beside the still slumbering James, I vowed that I would do my best to make sure it would become so.

9

Windsor Castle was one of the oldest of the royal residences, a fortress overlooking a strategic point of the Thames. Although Queen Elizabeth had liked it and stayed there often, it wasn't large enough to comfortably accommodate the households of both a king and a queen, and so our visits were few, usually only when James wanted to hunt in the extensive woodlands of its park. Sometimes I accompanied him on the hunt, which I enjoyed nearly as much as he did, finding rare moments of relief from the structures of my life as I galloped through the trees in pursuit of a beast. Afterward I always felt more competent to manage my responsibilities for having had the brief absence from them. But on this visit, although I was recovered from the strain of Sophia's birth, I still did not want to risk taking exercise which could be overly strenuous, and so I remained behind.

The hunts were scheduled in advance and changed only when the weather proved uncooperative, so the Secretary knew when to make his promised visit. He came one morning just after James and his courtiers had ridden out; a footman made his way to where I was sitting with my women on the North Terrace to tell me of his arrival. "My lord Secretary says he is here to discuss your plans for Somerset House," he said deferentially.

"Have him join us here," I said, pleased that so many of my attendants had heard the stated reason for the visit. As the footman hurried back inside the castle, one of my women said quietly, not intending for me to hear, "Cecil's too late for the hunt." Her voice had been sarcastic and derisive, sneering at the Secretary's bent and misshapen form. He never rode a horse, and the thought of him participating in the vigour of the hunt was cruel. I stood up and turned to look behind me, where a dozen or so of my younger women were gathered. My face showed my displeasure, and each of theirs looked anxious as I scanned them. But I would not be so strict as to insist upon finding the one who'd made the remark. "That comment was ugly. Whichever of you fails to understand that despite his appearance, the Secretary is one of the most powerful men in this land, the greater the fool is she."

I shooed them away as Cecil, accompanied by a small group of his clerks and assistants, emerged from the castle. He indicated for his attendants to remain at a distance and came to me, bowing. "Come, Mister Secretary," I said cordially, "let us walk the length of the terrace, while I tell you how I want mine redone at Somerset House." Side by side we walked out of hearing distance.

"There is a matter of English law I don't understand," I said when we were sufficiently far from the others, "relating to the succession."

We stopped by the low stone wall along the edge of the terrace, from where a long stretch of the Thames was visible down below. "It has been suggested to me that my children born in England might have greater claims to the English throne than the three born in Scotland. Is this so?"

His face was at first expressionless, but something in his eyes shifted, and I saw the alert mind behind the controlled poise. He had shed a small amount of his necessary political reserve, and I knew his answer would be honest.

He said, "Some would say so, Your Majesty. Not many, but some. But I believe most Englishmen now feel the barring of foreigners from the throne has become irrelevant through

King James's succession. There were other English candidates, but in the end, the English wanted him, despite his being Scottish. He also had the advantage of being male. After three queens, the people were ready for a king."

"Three queens?" Thinking only of Elizabeth and her sister Mary, I began to question him but stopped, remembering the sad fate of the young Jane, who had been deposed and executed after reigning for only nine days.

"Yes, including Queen Jane," he said, understanding where my thoughts had gone. "A great example of how so much depends on what the English people want in a sovereign. They didn't care that either Princess Mary or Elizabeth, or even both of them, were illegitimate. And so the same should be the case when God calls our present good king home to him, and there must be another. When I look into the future, I see little possible obstruction to Prince Henry's succeeding. He is already very popular here, and people talk of the great things he could accomplish as king. They see his displays of athleticism and horsemanship, and his easy authority among his peers in public, and they hear of his intellect and interest in martial strategy and politics. For them, he could be a leader victorious in wartime or in peaceful diplomacy, who would protect them. No matter what graces and talents your English-born daughter displays as she grows, it is unlikely she would be able to surpass the appeal of the prince as the next English sovereign."

I would have liked to hear that by law there was no obstacle to Henry's succeeding, but even if Cecil couldn't tell me so, his words were still reassuring. Of anyone in England, his opinion was underscored by experience. I began to feel relaxed in a way I hadn't since my conversation with Christian.

But an instant later, my barely new peace of mind vanished when the Secretary said, "The only impediment might be a second brother, born here. That, Your Majesty, might create a situation that could become a problem."

At once, I offered a swift silent prayer of thanks that my only living English child was a girl.

"Especially," Cecil added, very quietly and precisely, "if a rivalry were to develop between the brothers."

I looked out to the Thames, so far away that the boats and barges on it were the size of children's toys. Henry was already too old for toys; Christian had presented him with an actual warship. "My sons are not rivals," I said.

"The two princes are very different in character, and otherwise," Cecil replied. "They complement each other, which is fortunate for them, and you, and the king, and most of all for the kingdom. It is a terrible thing when claimants to a throne struggle with each other for it. It is little more than a century since the wars of Lancaster and York tore this country apart for thirty years."

I thought of how raptly Henry had stared at his new warship following us up the Thames. He would not easily relinquish what he already saw as his birthright. If challenged, even by a sibling, he would fight for what was his. "Those wars were between brothers?" I felt compelled to ask.

"Cousins. Two and a half centuries ago, the third King Edward left many children. All became powerful nobles, and their descendants eventually fought each other for the throne. There were too many claims." He gestured to the grey and beige walls of the castle, extending along the opposite side of the terrace as far as was visible in both directions. "It was that Edward who made a palace of this castle of Windsor. He sought to ensure his dynasty with many children. But it had an effect he had not foreseen. Even today, there are descendants from him with claims to the throne. But they are too diluted and distant now to ever come into serious consideration. For all of King Henry the Eighth's struggles to produce children, it was perhaps in the end a blessing he had so few." He paused, looking at the castle walls. "He's buried here, you know. Beneath the chapel."

"Yes," I said distractedly. "With Queen Jane Seymour."

"King James succeeded to the throne largely because there were so few other claimants close to the trunk of the royal family tree, and none — as the last queen was once heard to say — of sufficient power to rule satisfactorily."

Cecil started walking again as I did, continuing in the same direction as before, away from where our attendants were waiting.

"She liked it here at Windsor," he said easily. "She said it was the only one of her residences that could survive a siege. It was she who had this long terrace constructed into a permanent one for promenade and exercise." His tone changed. "She had a problem her ancestors hadn't had to contend with — religious divisions. She'd already experienced such issues after the death of her brother and during her sister's reign, and she understood how easily ambition could disguise itself within religion. And that problem, Your Majesty, might repeat itself should your children align themselves with different religions."

I started to stumble, and instantly he reached out to prevent me from falling, but it wasn't necessary. Given his slightness, he never would have been able to anyway. "My sons are not rivals," I said again, but with a touch less certainty than before.

"Not now," he replied. "Perhaps never, given their own characters. But they must always be aware that there are those who would use them for their own ambitions — who would welcome discord between them and make use of religious differences to create it. The future husbands of your daughters, also. You saw how the recent conspirators planned to use them. But that threat would always be so much less severe than what could come from a son. All too often, younger princes come to resent the fate which placed a brother in this world before them. It's understandable, when one thinks about it. To be so close to a throne, but not close enough, would be frustrating."

"It involves their temperaments," I said, still trying to avoid acknowledging to myself the full extent of the threat to Henry.

"And the wisdom of parents, which sometimes can mitigate or prevent rivalry. Our king has great wisdom, although at times certain subjects seem obscure for him. Perhaps this is one of them. He was, after all, an only child, with no siblings to contend with. But you, Your Majesty, have several, and I believe your experience might have given you a deeper ability to understand this matter than the king has. You can now take steps to decrease the likelihood of any future conflict over the succession."

"Such as?" I pressed.

"Ensuring a bond of friendship between your children grows strong, especially between the brothers. Steering your younger son towards talents and endeavours different from his brother's and not so much in the view of the public. Seeking careful marriages for your daughters, foreign ones without ambitions to press a claim here, but useful in terms of European politics. But most importantly, Your Majesty, there is a question you must ask yourself." He stopped and turned to look directly at my face. "Is your family complete?"

An instant passed before I understood that he was asking if I intended to have more children. I felt the urge to look away from his gaze, full of intelligence and foresight, but instead, I held it. The question could have been considered rude, for it was a subject no one else dared ask me about. But I understood that it cut through to the very centre of the issue. Charles wasn't English and Mary was female, and so both were unlikely to ever gather support for a challenging claim to the throne. But if I had English sons, they might.

"My last birth was difficult," I finally said.

He hesitated only slightly before agreeing. "Your recovery took longer."

"The doctors have said there is no reason to believe the next would be the same. But I am older now."

"And you already have four children." It was as close as he would dare come to saying I shouldn't have any more.

I'd found out what I'd needed to from him. But rather than setting my mind at ease, it had created new agitations and concerns. Most of all, it had made me see that an extremely important decision lay ahead of me.

"Thank you, Master Secretary," I managed to say. "You've given me much to consider. I am grateful and continue to regard you as a friend."

"I am honoured, Your Majesty. Please call upon me at any time."

"Now, let us finally talk of your beautiful house, so as to appear immersed in it by the time we reach our attendants." We turned and slowly started to walk back to them. I forced myself to talk of Theobalds, and the similar changes I wanted to make to Somerset House.

After he'd left, I returned to my suite and gave instructions that I was tired and not to be disturbed. I needed time alone to sort through the fears and hopes that now felt at odds with each other. I stayed in my bedroom for the rest of the day, mostly pacing the large but low-ceilinged, old-fashioned room, too agitated to remain in bed. Food was brought to me, but I barely touched it. Anna, seeing my mood, tried to remain with me, but I sent her out.

When James returned from the hunt, he sent a message inquiring how I was. In recent weeks I had made efforts to ensure I presented myself as being in robustly good health, but this time I replied that I was still feeling the aftereffects of dear Sophia's birth, and needed to rest appropriately. If I decided I was going to use fears of the detrimental effect on my health as a reason to avoid future childbirth, I might as well begin to set the stage for it now. Should I later decide against it, I could always change course.

Late in the day, weary from so many hours of anxious ruminating, I rested against one of the windows looking down into the large courtyard. It was busy with numerous people walking about, some in a leisurely manner and others hurriedly. Some had returned with James and still wore their riding garments. Across the courtyard was the large round tower perched on a little grassy hill, the original keep, the very heart of the castle that could still be protected should the outer walls be breached. It had always struck me as outdated, no longer necessary in a time when wars were fought differently and one seldom heard of long sieges. But then I remembered the peril we'd been in during the conspiracy, and how there'd been a few days when such a safe retreat would have been welcome. The thought of Henry as king years from now inside it, fending off an attack there came to mind, but I pushed it away. Thinking clearly was difficult enough without any more fearful speculations.

Beyond the round tower was the chapel, still out of view as it had been earlier when on the terrace Cecil had mentioned that

King Henry VIII was buried there. His presence could still be felt about the castle. Beneath the floor of the chapel, his remains lay alongside those of his third queen, Jane Seymour, who'd given him the son he'd so desired but had died doing so.

Below, in the courtyard, a colourfully dressed lady entered at the far end and started moving across, leading a few gentlewomen, the entourage marking her out as a noblewoman. Although too far away for me to recognise, she was still young, not yet middle-aged, judging by the lightness and agility with which she moved, and she walked with the grandeur of a countess or baroness. She was exactly the type of woman James would choose as a second wife should I die in childbirth, and who might give him more children — sons who would be English and could displace Henry as heir. The dynasty James and I had been ambitious to found in England would then continue with his descendants, but not mine.

Abruptly, I turned away from the window. It was beyond imaginable that all our efforts to join the English throne to that of Scotland for our descendants should in the end come to nothing for any of us except James. Years ago, I might have believed him too dedicated to our children to not try at all costs to prevent them being barred from the succession, but the self-absorption and withdrawal he'd displayed following the conspiracy now made me wonder if anything other than his own security as king mattered to him.

My decision was made: it was time for me to protect my children's future. I would go immediately to James and tell him we must view our family as complete, my reason being the possibility of detrimental or even fatal consequences for me if I had another child. It was best for me to go right now and talk to him, while his mood would be good from the hunt. Sending for him to come to me wouldn't do, for during even the slight delay my resolve might fade.

I was still wearing the dress I'd had on earlier when I'd met with the Secretary, as I'd been too preoccupied with my thoughts to change, although I had pulled off my jewellery, which now lay on the table where I'd thrown it carelessly. It had to be replaced, and my hair also needed adjusting before I could appear before James and whatever courtiers were with him before I took him aside. It would take mere seconds for my women to assist me, and I was about to call for them, when I looked at the bed in the centre of the room, its damask hangings pulled back and its covers and pillows neatly arranged, ready for me to occupy it. Since our arrival at Windsor, I'd thought that it might be time for James to resume coming to me at night — he had stopped when I'd found I'd been carrying Sophia. Now, as I looked at the bed, I wondered if I was ready to never have him return to it, or any other I occupied; to never again express our love physically. For that indeed was the only reliable way to ensure I never had a child again.

Frustrated and overwhelmed, I threw myself down on the bed. James, to my knowledge, had never had a mistress, despite both his grandfather and great-grandfather having fathered numerous children with women other than their queens. It was likely the austerity of his deeply held reformed beliefs were in part responsible, but also that he'd found his marriage bed satisfying. But he was still only forty, and were that bed to be denied him, I had to assume he would find solace in another.

Immediately, some part of me rejected that possibility, telling me that I still loved him and that stepping away from my place in his life would never be easy, if even possible. And I remembered all too well his downcast, silent mood of the previous months, rooted in suspicion that he would be removed and replaced. My withdrawing from him now might destabilise his peace of mind and his trust in his family, which had only recently been reestablished. That could have even worse consequences, causing him to reject Henry and the other children, along with myself.

Slowly, I sat up, pushing back my hair, which was now even more dishevelled. Sitting on the side of the bed, my feet touched the floor, which through my elegant slippers felt very smooth and stable. It had been foolish of me to have nearly run off to tell James something so important, especially since I now had concerns about whether I should. It would be far better for me to try to find another way to proceed. I needed to reconsider whether there was truly any substantial threat to Henry following James as king.

It was late in the day, the light at the window telling me it was nearly time for supper. Finally, I called out for my women, and when they came in, I asked if the king planned to sup in the banquet hall or in his rooms. They told me he would be in the banquet hall with the rest of the court and both our household staffs, since he had missed the midday meal because of the hunt. Everyone was already beginning to take their places.

"I'll join him," I said. "It's too late to change, but he won't know it's the same dress I've had on all day. And I doubt anyone would tell him. But please, fix my hair and jewellery."

Everyone in the crowded hall, including James, stood when the trumpet announced my entry and I appeared on the dais. "A welcome surprise," he said as he came and took my hand. "I'd thought you too unwell to attend." Behind him, courtiers and servants scurried to bring my chair forward to its usual place beside his.

"Some rest did me good," I answered. "And now I am fine."

Hearing this, the nearest courtiers, those chosen to sit on the dais, applauded. Following their example, everyone else did the same, although they were too far away to understand why, except for it having something to do with me.

I took my seat, James retook his, and everyone else in the hall sat down on their benches again. My women placed a napkin and my silver cutlery on the table before me, and a courtier set down a full finger bowl for me.

I turned to James. "The hunt was enjoyable?"

"Very much so. A little different, too. This time, the doe was as fleet as the stag. It provided interest."

Sometimes they are, I thought, but I didn't say so.

He smiled at me fondly. "Dear Anne, your presence was missed today. Hopefully you can join the next hunt."

"Perhaps," I answered uncertainly, although I returned his smile. There were important decisions to be made before acknowledging I was in good enough health to participate.

Trumpets sounded, announcing the first course. He said, "I heard you were visited by the Secretary today."

"I was. We spoke of Theobalds and the changes I want to make at Somerset House."

Bowls of pottage, with bread, were placed before us, and wine was poured into our silver cups. As I lifted mine, I remembered the tale of the drunkenness during the masque at Theobalds, where the Queen of Sheba had fallen to the floor. Had I not been recovering from childbirth, I would have been present, and the expensive and carefully prepared masque would have been appreciated instead of ruined. I set down the cup and said, "The Secretary is always so full of good ideas. He's given me much to think about."

James drank from his own cup, then said, "He always does, to our benefit. An important man to be sure, our new Earl of Salisbury."

I reached over and placed my hand on his, resting on the arm of his chair. "You were wise to express your appreciation so."

"He has earned our gratitude." He turned his hand over and briefly held mine before releasing it.

I leaned back in my chair and looked out at the packed benches of the long tables extending down the hall. "I'm thinking of changing the name of Somerset House to Denmark House."

More indifferently than not, James said, "Did he suggest it?"

"No," I answered. "It's a decision I must make by myself."

10

The next morning, having slept long and deeply after so many agitated hours the previous day, I felt better able to arrange my thoughts and priorities. But my concerns were still strong, and when I joined James for the morning prayers in St. George's Chapel, I was intensely aware of the two other kings besides Henry VIII buried there, Henry VI and Edward IV. Both had been central figures in the wars of York and Lancaster, whose future repetition, with religious conflict, was so feared by the Secretary. And although inside the chapel — more like a cathedral with its soaring ceiling and stained glass windows — everything was tranquil, outside on the roof were pinnacles with statues of many animals: lions, falcons, antelopes and others, all ferocious-looking and seemingly ready to fight to keep what was theirs. They were heraldic symbols of the various members of the Plantagenet family, descended from a king who'd had too many children. Sitting next to James, I bowed my head and prayed for divine guidance on what I should do regarding my own.

By the time we led our households back across the courtyards to the hall for breakfast, I was still undecided. James walked beside me, his steps uneven as they'd always been, but a little less awkward since he'd become heavier. Other than that, he'd aged surprisingly well; even the stresses of the past year had not taken much toll on his appearance or manner. At yesterday's supper some of the courtiers had told me how well he'd ridden during the hunt, with skill and agility, and how much he'd enjoyed it. His interest and enthusiasm for life was back again.

"We'll have the tournament intended for Christian's visit at the end of our stay here," he now said idly as we approached the hall. "So much effort and preparation for it shouldn't go to waste."

"Windsor Castle is a fitting setting for it," I remarked.

"The court requires diversions and entertainments. As do we all."

It occurred to me that perhaps it had been fortunate the tournament hadn't taken place while Christian had been here, without my presence. The results could have been disastrous if the drunkenness at the Theobalds masque had been repeated during the more vigorous activity. Even though the tips of the jousting lances were now padded to avoid injury, they could be dangerous, and the participants were no longer used to wearing the heavy armour of earlier generations. Although all were strong young men, they were often clumsy in it. Today's tournaments were for spectacle only, but as such could still be splendidly memorable events.

"We must have the children attend," I said. "They would surely enjoy it, especially Henry. Our family seated together in the lists would make quite the impression on the crowds."

"Yes," he agreed, mildly. "Quite the impression. Mary must be included, a reminder for all that we have an English child as well as our Scottish ones."

The remark was startling in its relevance to my concerns, and I wondered if in some way he'd learned of them. A quick look at his face told me he hadn't, and what he'd said had been random, of the moment. And yet it also told me that he had previously given it thought.

I said steadily, "In a few years, perhaps Henry can participate with the knights. Of course, the others would have to let him win, and everyone would be very careful. But it could publicly present him in the role of a strong and capable warrior, should England need one. The people should feel their future is secure."

He was silent for a little too long before answering, "Their security lies not on the battlefield but in peaceful negotiations and alliances. Learning how to achieve them is how our son can reign effectively as the future king, not by appearing to excel in some contrived pastime."

His tone, although gentle, had been corrective in a way I hadn't liked. But I would overlook it since he'd implied the expectation that Henry would be king.

Later that morning, when I was alone in my room with Anna, I said reflectively, "James tries to see himself in Henry. He thinks that he would reign the same way he has and continue his legacy of peace. But James has been fortunate that neither Scotland nor England has needed to defend themselves against aggressors while he's been king. Who knows what the future might hold? These religious conflicts can easily become war, like the Spanish war with England in the time of the last queen."

"The prince's talents are different from his father's," she replied. "God gives gifts to those he sends to sit upon thrones according to what challenges he intends them to face."

"And what of Charles? His gifts are different from his brother's — more similar to James's." I went to the window overlooking the courtyard and looked across to the round tower again. "You don't think James might favour him as he grows older, do you?"

"No, if you mean as successor. King James values tradition and must understand it was what brought him to both his thrones. He must believe it only right for Henry as eldest son to succeed him. Even should he grow to like Charles better, he would not change that. He knows that God shows his intent in such things through the divine order in which children are born."

I turned away from the window to face her. "Do you think Charles might ever challenge Henry for the throne, in years to come? I fear he will be manipulated by others, especially through religion. We already saw that the conspirators planned to use Elizabeth so." Remembering Anna's Catholic sympathies, I refrained from mentioning that it had been a plan of the Catholics.

She answered, "Until now, Charles has been too young for you to assess whether or not it would be in his character to attempt it. But he is almost seven, and you might now be able to." She pushed a few loose strands of hair back under her bonnet. "I have no children, and their ways are mysterious to me. But it does seem to me that they must care for and respect each other. I'm sure that if you talked with Charles, you'd find him already respectful of his brother's position, and it would set your fears to rest."

I would do so, in the near future. It was entirely possible that my fears about Henry being challenged by a sibling were ungrounded. A conversation with Charles might yield an indication of whether they were or not, and help me decide if having additional children might be the best path for all of us.

The opportunity to speak with him came about during the final plans for the tournament, when arrangements were being made for the children. They were to come to Windsor Castle that morning, where James and I would receive them ceremoniously before going to the lists outside. I sent a message to Charles's guardian that I wished him to arrive very early, before the others, so that I could have a private meeting with him. I wanted, I said, to see how his education and social skills were progressing. As I wished to do so without James present, I had deliberately chosen a time when I knew he'd be occupied with the many important guests for the tournament.

Charles more than any of us had improved since coming to England, but largely because he had most needed to. In Scotland, despite extensive and expensive attentions, he had remained frail, and I had often thought it wouldn't be long before he followed his deceased siblings into the vault in Holyrood. He'd arrived in England at age three still barely able to talk and walk. James had placed him under the guardianship of Sir Robert Carey, a Boleyn cousin of the last queen, and rumoured to be an illegitimate descendant of King Henry himself.

Sir Robert and his wife Dame Elizabeth had exerted themselves, though I did not know whether this was out of ambition to ingratiate themselves with us or genuine kind interest in the sorry little duke now in their care. It had been reported to us that every day Charles had been coaxed into playing while wearing heavy but comfortable boots of Spanish leather and brass specially made for him, which had strengthened his legs and ankles, and both Careys had spent hours encouraging him to talk. The results had been dramatic, and my weak son had begun to flourish in ways I never would have believed possible back in Scotland. Although at times he stammered, he now spoke readily to both James and myself when he visited. Last time we'd seen him, with his siblings at Greenwich, he had told us Sir Robert was starting to teach him how to ride and hunt, and had promised to teach him to shoot as well. But at the mention of shooting, I had quickly changed the subject, for any talk of gunpowder around James was still best avoided.

In London, the Careys occupied apartments with Charles at Whitehall, and shortly after dawn on the morning of the tournament they arrived with him, accompanied by his tutor and a few attendants. As they entered my sitting room, Charles, at the head of the small group, walked not only easily but with perfect posture, stopping and bowing low a few steps in front of where I sat, the Careys and the others behind him curtseying or bowing also. Although small, he was clearly the central figure in the group, an English Duke of York and a Scottish Duke of Albany with royal status, of which it was immediately apparent he was very much aware. It surprised me, for although I recognised his manner of wearing royalty like a garment from having seen it in Henry, I'd never before noticed it in Charles. But for a long time, I'd seen him only in the company of Henry or Elizabeth, where he blended in, with no reason to feel himself more special because of his birth. It was reassuring that with his brother and sister, he knew his correct place.

The bow over, he stayed where he stood and said formally, "It is an honour to be asked for by you, Your Majesty, my mother."

On either side behind him, the Careys hovered a little protectively. They were clearly proud of the good impression Charles was already making. Anywhere else they would have been thought to be his parents — an easy mistake, for both of them were the right age, about the same as James and myself, and they had the same dark hair as Charles. Surprisingly, I felt a touch of regret and jealousy that I hadn't felt for years. I'd missed the opportunity to bring my child to health and strength, the way the woman standing behind him could now claim to have done. Had I been able to do so myself, I might not have felt the alienation and disappointment I always had.

The love I felt for him, distant and formal, might instead have been immediate and unguarded in expression, like that which now seemed to flow to him from Dame Elizabeth. It was almost unbearable for me to see, and I looked away from her.

"Come, Charles," I said, standing and extending my hand towards him. He hesitated only slightly, then came forward and, after removing his glove, shyly took my hand and held it.

To the Careys, I said, "Your efforts have yielded fine results. I have so much to thank you for." Almost imperceptibly, the little hand in mine relaxed its grip. Charles was pleased I approved of them. He liked them, perhaps even loved them. I could only wonder what he felt towards me and James.

The Careys murmured some deferential response about always being available to serve their sovereigns, and I smiled at them gratefully. I was sure they would have liked to talk with me further, but I had little enough time to spend with Charles and wanted to get on with it. Looking at Dame Elizabeth, I asked, "He's breakfasted, hasn't he?"

"Yes, Your Majesty," she answered, "several hours ago. I made sure he was fortified for the trip here on the Thames. We left in the dark, and the river breezes can still be strong then."

"I'd never been in a boat at night before," Charles said in a small voice. Both Careys instantly looked at him with concerned expressions, and I felt his hand tense. Although protocol prohibited courtiers from initiating conversation with James or myself, the Careys likely had been uncertain as to what rules applied within our family circle, and had told Charles to wait until I spoke first.

"Our children speak to us as they wish," I said, feeling I was asserting myself as a mother. I'd been pleased he'd been comfortable enough to do so. "I've had some sweets prepared for us," I told Charles. "It's long enough after breakfast, and a while yet until dinner. I'm looking forward to them myself."

There was an adjacent small room where I could dine privately when I didn't want to go to the hall, and I'd already had some confections sent there. I dismissed the Careys, requesting that they stay available with the tutor in case I had questions, and telling my women to see that they were made comfortable in one of the anterooms. As they walked backward out of my presence, I could almost feel Charles wishing he could go with them.

"We have marzipan and sugar treats, and apple and honey pastries," I said as I led him into the room where they were spread out on the little table. On either side of it were two chairs, one with a large cushion, which, waving away the footman ready to assist him, he easily climbed onto himself, after I was seated. But he did allow his footman to push his chair further in as the one attending me did the same. As I'd instructed, both then left, closing the door behind them.

The room felt very domestic and cozy, with colourful tapestries, and although there was a fireplace the weather was still mild enough not to require it, and the candelabras were unnecessary because the single window gave enough natural light. But across the courtyard the round tower was even more visible than it was from my bedroom, and because of the way we were seated it appeared to loom behind Charles, distractingly. I wished I'd chosen a different place, but it was too late to move elsewhere. I exhaled deeply and relaxed back in my chair.

Across from me, Charles sat still, his hand folded and resting on the table. His manners were good; he'd been taught to wait. "Go ahead and have what you like," I said, gesturing to the full silver trays. "I'd asked for some sweetened pears also. But they're not in season yet."

"I've been taught we must be patient for things," he answered. "But it's difficult sometimes." Very politely he washed his fingers in the bowl of water and meticulously dried them on the accompanying napkin. Then, he studied the trays, looking at each pastry or confection. Already, I felt I was learning that his nature was careful and methodical, and I liked it. He hadn't grabbed for what he wanted, without giving himself the time to decide what he would prefer the most. It was charming to see signs of the type of man he'd become. Again, I felt the loss I had earlier, for I was confronting the extent to which I had been distanced from the everyday lives of my children.

Finally, he decided what he wanted, and carefully took it and placed it on the plate before him. Then he looked at me. "You're not having any?"

So he was thoughtful of others as well. I smiled and said kindly, "Not right now. I intended them for you. You can have one or two more if you like."

He began to eat the pastry. Halfway through, he paused. "Do you have more for Henry?" he asked.

"Yes, when we dine. And for Elizabeth too. She likes sweets very much."

"But not for Mary?" He eyed me seriously.

"No, she's still too young."

"I was wondering if there'd be enough for all of us."

"I can assure you, there are."

"I'll have another then, after this." He smiled contentedly, finished the pastry, and selected a confection. It was a pretty thing, made of white marzipan and sugar, with blue stripes.

"Do you think there's fruit inside?" he asked. "Sometimes the inside is different from what you see outside."

"You'll have to find out." It was exactly what I was doing with him, attempting to learn about what lay beneath his perfect manners. So far, I was seeing a child of steady disposition, sensitive to those around him.

He hesitated, holding the confection. "How many is Henry to be allowed?"

Something about this question sounded deeper. "I don't know. I haven't given it thought. The same as you, I suppose."

His eyes widened in surprise. "The same? Not more?"

"No."

Looking very satisfied, he smiled, then swiftly ate the confection entirely.

The way he did so did not match his manner up until that point. I waited until he was finished, then asked quietly, "Why would you think Henry might have more than you?"

"Because he is older. And he is to become king."

It was what I had wanted to find out, his attitude towards his siblings, especially Henry. He had gone right into it with no prompting from me. But I wondered whether it was good that it was so present in his thoughts, especially with the shift in his tone.

I asked, "Do you think he's going to make a good king?"

"Yes," he answered at once, to my great relief. But an instant later I sat up very tensely in my chair as he added, "But I could too."

"There can only be one king," I said abruptly.

He became very still again. "I have been told my father the king once thought to have Henry become king in England and me in Scotland." He sighed, and his face showed disappointment. "But he changed his mind. He now wishes for it to become one country, Great Britian. And so, there is to be need for only one king. Henry."

"One king," I repeated.

Suddenly, he was angry. He picked up his napkin and crumpled it between both his hands. "It's not fair. I see him all the time, and I do my best to copy his ways, even though I'm smaller and not as strong as he is. He always says how much I improve. He's kind to me and shows me affection, like the Careys. So, I thought that if I asked him to make me king of Scotland when he became king of England, he would say yes. But he didn't! He even laughed. He barely ever laughs at anything, you know."

"Yes," I said, so disturbed I was barely able to speak. "I know."

He still clutched the napkin, as though holding something of great importance. "He laughed and said no, that could never be. He said that I would be a clergyman, or chancellor, or foreign ambassador, and that I would be a great help to him, and both England and Scotland. But that I would never be a king."

With effort, I prevented myself from harshly replying that indeed he never would be, that it was his brother's birthright. I looked away from him, down to the trays of sweets. As I did, very quickly, his little hand swept out and took another. I wondered if he might try to grab the throne from Henry in the same way.

My face must have shown dislike, for I heard him say uncertainly, "You said I could have two more. This is the second."

"Yes, go ahead." I forced myself to look up and smile at him. While he ate it, I tried to push away all the thoughts of the wars of York and Lancaster that had rushed in upon me, and of siblings and relatives fighting each other for the throne. It was a time for decisions, not anxious speculations. I would speak to the Careys and to Charles's tutor, expressing my displeasure that he had been told of the brief, passing thought of James's to leave the Scottish throne to him, and directing that he be educated with examples of civil wars and how religion could agitate politics. I would also see that he and Henry were more often together so that their fraternal bond was strengthened. Eventually, when Henry began to take a role in government and court life, Charles would be placed in his care in his household. Surely whatever resentments he felt over his secondary position could be overcome. I began to feel less apprehensive about any future problems coming from him. Even if there were any, there was little chance he would be preferred by anyone over Henry. He was, like him, Scottish by birth, not English.

Charles finished the confection, wiped his hands on the now crumpled napkin, then folded it and placed it neatly on the table. My thoughts now better composed, I asked, "So, you understand, don't you, that what Henry told you was correct? That your position as second son is important, but you'll never be king?"

"Yes." He placed a hand on the napkin in a childishly resolved way.

"I know it must be a disappointment. But we all have disappointments to contend with in life. As with so many things, the ones that come to those in our position as a ruling family are greater."

"Henry said the same. He said he'd like nothing better than to sail the oceans and discover new lands. But he'll never be able to, because he must become king instead. And it seemed to me that he didn't want to be king at all." Again, he sighed.

Then he looked at me and said, "There wasn't any surprise inside."

"Inside?" I asked, not understanding him. "Inside of what?"

He pointed to the sweets. "Inside the pastries. These were the same inside as out."

A few remained on the trays, beside the empty places of the ones Charles had chosen. He'd been respectful in taking only what he'd been told he could have. But if I had more sons, English ones, I wondered if they'd do the same.

An hour later I sat formally beside James in his large, crowded to overflowing reception room, with Charles next to me as Henry arrived and made his way down the central aisle, to exuberant cheers and applause from the courtiers. After greeting us he smoothly and naturally took Charles by the hand and led him to sit next to him, on the other side of James. Elizabeth then entered, to a similar welcome, fulfilling anyone's expectations as the image of a beautiful young princess. She serenely made her greetings and took her place beside me. But the largest and most enthusiastic response came as Mary appeared, carried by her guardian, who gently set her down and held her hand down the aisle. Mary, a lovely child with large blue eyes, a pink complexion and fair hair, was unintimidated by suddenly becoming the centre of attention as the delighted courtiers strained forward and jostled with each other to see her. She looked proudly eager to display her new walking skills. Halfway down the aisle she let go of her guardian's hand, laughed merrily, and ran the rest of the way to us. James, dropping all formality, went and picked her up, giving her an affectionate kiss, which she immediately returned, wrapping her little arms around his neck. The cheers and applause that followed were the loudest yet, seeming to shake Windsor

Castle's walls.

Even at slightly less than a year and a half, Mary had naturally known how to charm the crowd and make the most of her moment. As her mother I was as charmed as anyone else, and pleased by the excellent impression she had made, but my satisfaction was tempered by my earlier conversation with Charles. It was possible the reason for her being best received was because she was English, the first royal English child born in seventy years. She represented little threat to Henry's succeeding, for as a female, it was unlikely she'd ever be chosen to replace him. I'd heard often enough since arriving in England that after half a century of queens, the people had been ready for a man on the throne again, and had been pleased he'd arrived with two princes for the future. But as I stared out past James and Mary to the still responding crowd, I became convinced that if he held a young English prince instead, that child might be preferred. And I knew then that my decision regarding whether or not to have more children was made. My family would remain complete as it now was.

Trumpets sounded outside, calling us to the lists for the tournament to begin. I took Mary from James, and with the other children behind us, we led the way to the courtyard, where coaches waited to convey us through the nearby gate to the lists. A great wave of excitement from the following courtiers seemed to sweep us into our four-horse coach, the largest and most ornate, with very large windows for us to be easily seen. We were the royal family on full display in our fine outfits and jewelled and plumed hats, and after we'd passed through the gate and over the bridge, roaring and jubilant crowds wanting to see us lined the short route from the castle to the lists.

"So many people!" Elizabeth exclaimed. "They must have come from miles around!"

"It's free," James said, looking out the windows at the crowds on either side. "Unlike those in the reign of Queen Elizabeth. Even though it's expensive, I wanted the people to know we appreciate them. Most have never seen a tournament. And many have never seen us."

"I doubt they'll all fit in the lists," Henry said. "They're likely full already." To his brother, he said, "Sit forward a little more so they can see you."

Charles did so at once. At the same time, I heard him tell Henry in a low voice, "There are sweets for you after dinner. She had some for me."

With no change of expression, Henry replied, "You shouldn't refer to Her Majesty our mother as 'she'."

James, not having heard the exchange, was telling Elizabeth, "Don't just scan the crowd as we pass, pick out individual faces to look at directly. They'll all still feel included, but some especially so. And they'll talk of it afterwards."

I held Mary standing on my lap, so she could be seen and admired. Again, she smiled and appeared to enjoy the excitement of the new experience. Frequently, intermingled with the cries of "God Save King James!" I could make out the rest of our names, but most of all Mary's. The response to her from the common folk along the route was the same as it had been from the nobility and gentry inside. The decision I'd come to was the right one: there would be no more princes or princesses in our family.

Henry looked at James and said again, "All of these people aren't going to find places to see the tournament."

James answered, "They know that. They would have come earlier and found places nearer the lists entrance if they'd wanted to. No, these people have chosen to see us instead. There aren't many opportunities for all six of us to be seen together, with a chance to see the newest princess. It's important for them. Years from now they'll tell their children how they saw the entire royal family in their coach outside Windsor Castle."

I looked out the window on my side and smiled. But I didn't focus on individual faces, seeing instead only a great passing blur of them, and many waving hands. Even so, I heard a distinct shout from the crowd above the din of the other voices: "She smiled at me! The queen smiled at me!" It was followed by others shouting, "God save Queen Anne and her children!" Immediately, I was drawn from the future back to the moment. James was right about it being the only time we had all been on display together, and being so now filled me with a sense of accomplishment. I had succeeded in my most important function as queen in having created a royal family.

The coach stopped as we pulled up to the back of our stand in the lists, and a footman opened the door. The Countess of Bedford was waiting, and immediately reached in and took Mary from me. As she stepped back, other courtiers and attendants pushed in to help us out and accompany us inside. There would be only so much room in our stand behind us, and everyone wanted to be seen there. As I stepped from the coach, behind me I heard Charles asking Henry, "If you don't want all your sweets, can I have one?"

"If you share it with our sisters," he answered.

"She said Mary's too young."

"Don't call her she."

We went up a narrow set of wooden steps and entered the lists. Inside, the enclosed rectangular field looked very different from its nondescript exterior, the stands already crammed with spectators, with banners and awnings above and the walls below colourfully painted as elaborate tapestries. A great roar of welcome went up as we appeared and took our seats, James and I on elaborate chairs designed to resemble thrones.

Trumpets sounded, and the participating jousters, all splendid in medieval armour and with intricately decorated shields, and lances, then rode into the tiltyard. They went around it in a great procession, finally arriving where we sat, where each bowed to us from his horse. James and the children were delighted by the spectacle, but it was all I could do to continue smiling and make a show of enjoyment. Although the armour and weapons were merely part of pageantry, for me they were stark reminders of times of war and conflict, and the battles of York and Lancaster which had been so much on my mind of late.

11

The following day, after the children had all left Windsor, and the lists outside the castle were being taken apart, I sent a message to James requesting he come to my rooms. It was at a time when he could easily comply, before riding out on a hunt with several of the nobles who had stayed on in Windsor — better for him to not retreat to the solitude of his room or study after our conversation. Briefly, I had considered delegating the talk to one of my doctors, but had decided against it. If we were never to lie with each other again as man and wife, it was something I should tell him myself.

I remained in my bed, where I'd lingered all morning, not because I was still tired from the exertions of the previous day, but because it was one of the few places where I could be alone with my thoughts. My women had attended morning prayers without me, and breakfast had been brought, although I'd barely touched it. When the plates had been cleared away, I'd had the bed curtains drawn back and a new robe of green satin arranged by my women around my shoulders. After I'd had them remove my night bonnet and arrange my hair neatly against the pillow behind me, I had them bring a mirror. Against the dark green robe my complexion looked clear and beautiful, but very pale. Satisfied that I didn't look overly robust, I waved the mirror away. James already knew it had taken me longer than ever before to recover from my last childbirth, but I didn't want the way I looked to contradict my claim that I didn't feel strong enough to undergo it again. That decision would not be seen as strange, anyway. I would be thirty in a few months, and seen as starting to age; by forty most people were considered old. It would be a change, but James and I would find other ways to maintain the bond between us.

"Are you unwell?" he asked as soon as he came in and saw me still in bed. As I expected, he was already dressed in a riding outfit. For the first time, he looked a little old for one, and I wondered if his skill and dexterity in both riding and hunting had been maintained. But his courtiers and attendants would be protective and humour him, allowing him to maintain the illusion that he still excelled where he did not. My women told me often that my beauty hadn't diminished as I'd aged, but I'd known it to be flattery.

"Only tired. I'm no longer used to doing as much as I did yesterday." Behind where he stood at the foot of the bed, across the room, Anna stood watching me. I gestured towards the door, and she wordlessly summoned the gentlewomen sitting by the window and ushered them out. Behind the closed door I could hear their laughter as they met James's gentlemen in the outer room.

"I'd hoped you might be able to join us when we rode out today," he said. "It's been months since you have."

I hadn't since before the gunpowder conspiracy, which now seemed part of a different lifetime. So much had changed since those halcyon days following Mary's birth. I sighed and looked away from him sadly. "It's going to be some time before I can do that again."

"Whatever suits you, dearest Anne. Your wellbeing is paramount." He smiled kindly, then came around to the side of the bed and sat facing me, leaning back against the cushion of the curtains gathered at the bedpost. I drew back a little more against the pillow. The conversation had gone exactly where it had needed to, and I knew I should take advantage of the moment and tell him what I had to. Yet I hesitated, suddenly doubting my decision. Anxiety stirred in me, and my back become damp with perspiration.

He continued, "What an excellent time we had at the tournament, didn't we?"

"We so rarely have the opportunity to all be seen together in public."

"I was so pleased by the enthusiasm the children showed for the adventure of it, all of them, even little Mary. Charles's especially was satisfying, for it showed promise of an unexpected martial ability that might equal Henry's. His time with the Careys has been most rewarding."

Never before had he said anything like it, and I was startled. But the experience of the conspiracy could have changed him. "You have always been a man of peace, James!" I reminded him. "How often have you said your greatest ambition would be to bring peace to Europe? I'd even thought you'd hoped for Henry to be more of the scholar you are."

"His intellect is more than satisfactory, and other talents can only enhance it. After yesterday, I see I can have hopes for the same in Charles. And it would not displease me for our daughters to have an understanding of military matters also. Queen Elizabeth made a great impression on her troops when she rode out and rallied them as the Armada arrived off these shores. My mother would have benefitted from greater ability and experience. The one time she needed to lead her own forces in the field, she failed woefully, despite having the larger army."

"She'd fought against her own brother, had she not?" I asked quietly, remembering.

"Half-brother, the Earl of Moray. Losing that battle caused her flight into England, which turned out so unfortunately for her."

It was exactly the type of fraternal conflict I was convinced our children needed to be steered away from. Henry alone should be the warrior, capable of holding his throne from anyone who would try to take it from him. For years, I had encouraged Henry to understand that being king was to be his place in the world, and he would need to have the skills and ability to do so. He'd accepted it, putting away his hopes of world exploration and adventure. It was absolutely necessary that the choices I now made continued in support of his having and keeping his rightful place. The doubt which had taken me a moment ago vanished. I sat up as straight as possible. "There is something important I have to speak to you about. It's why I asked for you today."

"Ah," he said, with only the mildest concern. "And what would that be?"

"I have come to the conclusion that further childbearing would affect my health in ways that could be very detrimental," I replied firmly. "James, I do not feel we should lie together as man and wife any longer." I paused, but only long enough for my words to register with him. "Such a change, of course, would sadden me deeply. But I must ensure that I maintain not only my health but perhaps my very life, to fulfil my other responsibilities as a wife, a mother, and as a queen. In seeking to preserve myself, I am setting others before me."

Except for a slight lowering of his eyelids, there was no change in his expression. But even that tiny gesture told me he had been taken by surprise. Gently, I said, "Surely you saw how difficult a time I had with Sophia. I —"

"Anne." He stopped me, waving one of his hands before him. "You need say no more. Do you imagine that for one moment I would question this? I actually feel remiss in not having thought this through myself. Certainly, this has now become a necessary change for us. It would be foolish and irresponsible to do otherwise, especially since we have four children."

"Thank you," I said softly, resting back on the pillows. I was relieved he had not withdrawn into the same silence the conspiracy had brought upon him. The time I had chosen had been the right one, directly after the success of yesterday's tournament, with the demonstrated good feeling of the crowds towards him.

"You have nothing to thank me for," he said, leaning forward and placing a hand over mine. "No man has a better wife, no king a better queen. I look forward to the many years of close companionship ahead of us."

His words were the best I could have hoped for, but something about the way he'd spoken of the future suggested a long succession of empty days without meaning. Swiftly, the doubt returned, this time with a feeling that I was on the point of the decision becoming unchangeable, and that we should still talk further. I tried to think of something to say that would take us back into the conversation, but could not.

He stood up, seeming to move more slowly and awkwardly than when he'd come in, like a much older man. For all the smoothness of his response to my news, it had affected him. Perhaps he too had envisioned the same series of vacant days that I had. Yet if either of us was to say anything else in the few remaining moments before he left, to reconsider, I would have to be the one to do it. But within me, I found nothing but silence.

He came closer and kissed me on the forehead. "Dearest Anne," he then said. "I do hope you'll be able to ride with us at least once before we leave Windsor. If not, perhaps we can have an excursion sometime before the winter snows begin. Somewhere you might particularly want to go." He thought for a moment. "We could visit Secretary Cecil at Theobalds, for you to gather further ideas for your changes at Somerset House."

"That would be nice. How thoughtful of you to suggest it." His talking of inconsequential things seemed carefree, but from years of familiarity I knew he was simply avoiding the more serious matter, until he'd had time to fully adjust to it. It was best for me to follow his lead, as though nothing of importance had just occurred. "Denmark House, its new name."

"Most fitting. I'm sure you'll be spending a great deal of time there." He looked away quickly, as though something had drawn his attention. "Yes," he said as he looked back to me. "I think we should try to visit the Secretary's home sometime this autumn."

With that, he left. As I watched the door close behind him, I wondered if he somehow knew it had been the Secretary's advice that had helped me reach my decision.

12

One of the things I liked best about Denmark House was the open space of the terrace between the house and the Thames, different from the other mansions of the Strand closer to, or directly on, the riverbank. The man who'd built it in the last century, the Duke of Somerset, had sought a new style still apparent not only in the terrace but the size and shape of the mansion's rooms and many windows. It had appealed to me the first time I'd entered, suggesting not so much a blank canvas but one with an already pleasing painting I could bring to further beauty with my own aesthetic. I had spent the last five years changing it in ways that enhanced and expanded the duke's original vision. As I sat on a clear and cloudless late April morning in 1612 beside one of the large windows in my bedroom parlour overlooking the terrace, I was certain the duke would have approved of my work.

Behind me I heard movement, and a few yards away where my women were seated, I saw them look up towards the door, but without surprise, telling me someone familiar had come in. A moment later Anna appeared beside me.

"The Prince of Wales is here," she said, looking a trifle displeased by his arrival. She didn't have to ask if I'd expected him, for she knew my schedule to its smallest detail, and had known I had not.

Anyone else I would have seen arrive, because they all came and went by the Thames, and from where I sat I had a view of the river steps. But Henry, now eighteen and formally participating in the government, had his own household and court at St. James's Palace, and since it wasn't directly on the river, he always rode through the city when he visited me. The surprise was a pleasant one. I was already fully dressed and ready for visitors, as was my custom each day, whether I expected them or not. "Show him up here, please, Anna. Is he alone? Or is Charles with him?"

Charles lived in Henry's household, where Henry had responsibility for him. James had placed him there at my request, and now at age eleven the results had been satisfying. His current situation was a subtle improvement upon what the Careys had offered as guardians, especially in his learning how to fit in with the royal family. Of greatest importance to me was the fact that the brothers had become friends, and Charles often accompanied Henry when he went out. But today, Henry had come alone, telling me it was a matter of some importance.

"Take advantage of this fine day and walk on the terrace," I told the women. Looks of disappointment came over all their faces, for they were mostly young and unmarried, and Henry, in addition to being the as yet unengaged heir to the throne, was handsome, with appealing self-assurance somehow enhanced by his always serious manner. But they did as I told them, although slowly, no doubt hoping to at least pass Henry as he came in. In their white livery, only recently switched from the winter red after Easter, they looked like a great cloud as they went out. I wondered if they would go to the riverbank to watch the passing boats, or the orangery, or bring some of the dogs out to play with.

There was a formal knock at the door, and I heard it open. "The Prince of Wales, Your Majesty," Anna announced.

I kept my seat, not turning, and she ushered him into view next to me. She stepped back as he bowed, then knelt on one knee as I extended my hand, which he kissed. "Your Majesty, my mother," he said.

"Dispense with the formalities," I replied, smiling. He rose and kissed my cheek, and we quickly embraced.

Although he did not quite smile in return — he still seldom did — the look on his face became easier, more relaxed. But an instant later it changed again as he stood back up and stared at Anna. It was a look I'd seen him give her before, and it disturbed me. She saw it too, and her own face became masklike as she turned her eyes to the floor.

"Leave us, Anna," I said quietly. We waited silently as she went out, then I turned to Henry. "Be kinder to her. She sees your —" I hesitated, searching for the right word — "disapproval."

"She cannot possibly believe the papist nonsense," he said dismissively. "She uses it to make herself feel special. So tolerated by the queen, she must be important."

"Her belief runs deeper than that. You must be more tolerant of our Catholic subjects, Henry." I waved my hand. "Enough of Anna. You haven't come here to talk of her, I assume?"

"Of course not."

"Bring a chair and sit with me."

He went and got one of the farthingale chairs from where the women had been sitting and pulled it before me, so he could face me with his back to the window. As he did, I saw the women emerge into view on the lawn below, their billowing dresses white against the green grass as they started walking towards the river. Faintly through the closed window I could hear their laughter and lively talk. Henry noticed them as well, but did not react; he simply turned away and sat down.

"Elizabeth would so easily fit in with them," I said. "How I wish I could have had her with me as she grew up. I've missed so much of her childhood and youth. Each time I saw her, it was like she had jumped into an older version of the child I was expecting. I think that's why I feel so aged myself."

He sat straight on the chair with his hands resting on the black satin of his breeches, below his matching black leather and velvet doublet. "My lady mother, thirty-seven is not old. You do not look old, either."

"I said how I feel, not how I look. I know I am well preserved. But I do believe I would have retained more of my youthful feeling had Elizabeth been at my side over the years." With Henry, I tended to talk more than I did with most people, because he was so often silent. "You and Charles lived closer, but it's different for a mother and daughter. Even so, I would have raised all of you had I had my way. Your father absolutely refused. It was a matter of great contention between us following your birth. Eventually, I gave in, as I needed to for political reasons and for your father's peace of mind. The legacy of the discord — hatred, even — between his own parents weighed on him, and I needed to do what I could to reassure him it was different with us. Such are the decisions one must make when a queen. I don't regret it. But I do feel a certain loss in having been so distant from my daughter." I sighed. "Sometimes I wonder if Mary would have been closer to me if she had lived."

Mary's remains now lay with her infant sister Sophia's, in Westminster Abbey. She had died of pneumonia at age two and a half, having been taken ill shortly after our triumphant family gathering at the Windsor tournament in 1606. For a year she had improved, but then faded again, during which time I had made repeated trips to her household to provide what comfort I could. The ending, although expected, had been devastating for me, especially since James by necessity had been away in the north. Her death had seemed particularly cruel, her birth having been such a celebration of our arrival in England, the beginning of a new era not just for us but for everyone in the country. Years ago, I had started the custom of saving a trinket in memory of each child I'd lost, and I had done so with Mary. But this time, as I'd put the small container of them away, I'd known it would be a long time before I could look at them again.

Mary's loss had been met with sad silence by Henry, instead of the more visible grief of the rest of us, even James. But it was typical of him not to show his feelings, a trait that had become more pronounced as he'd grown older. Now, he made no comment on her and changed the subject. "I'm here to speak with you of Elizabeth."

He sounded very grave, and I felt myself tense. One of the few times he and I had ever seriously quarrelled had been six months ago over the possibility of Elizabeth marrying the newly widowed Spanish king. James had decided she should be married at sixteen, and since she was now fifteen, discussions of potential marriages had deepened in the past year. Various matches with both Reformed and Catholic royalty had been considered, as others were for Henry.

For years I'd held out hopes for Henry's marriage to the Spanish princess, but they had now vanished with news of her imminent betrothal to the young king of France. When the Spanish queen had unexpectedly died, there had been immediate interest in Elizabeth. The prospect of my daughter being queen of the most important empire on earth had thrilled me and had appeared entirely possible. King Philip being twenty years her senior had not seemed a serious impediment, for such marriages were common not only in royal but noble families, and were often successful personally as well as politically. That he was widely known to be of a mild and gentle disposition was also in his favour. Although I had years ago resolved not to meddle in English politics, I had gone so far as to make my feelings known to James, who had listened but refrained from promising a commitment. Then, I had very quietly met with the Spanish ambassador to make my interest known.

But Henry's opposition had been unmoving from the first. When the Spanish had said they would expect Elizabeth to change her religion, he had publicly stated his opinion that it would approach treason for anyone in England or Scotland to support the marriage. Henry had already made a substantial impression in Parliament and among the people, and was regarded as someone to be respected and deferred to, as he would one day be king. Indeed, there were loose but recognisable factions around him and James, one representing the old ways, the other the new. Awkward situations sometimes came about, showing which side someone favoured. Last summer during a hunt James had publicly criticised Henry's hunting ability, causing him to turn and ride away. Half the courtiers had gone with him, half remaining with James. It had been up to me to mediate the little rift, which both had been eager to resolve. But it had made Henry's increasing influence obvious, and a few months later when he'd taken his stand against the Spanish marriage, I'd known it was doomed unless I could persuade him to change his mind.

At first, I'd been fairly confident I'd be able to, with effort, and had invited him to dine with me. He'd listened politely to my arguments, including the possibility of Elizabeth's eventually being able to quietly establish a foothold for Reformed religion in Spain. But we had not even been halfway through when I'd noticed he'd said nothing, and that he'd tasted neither food nor drink. When I'd asked whether he'd prefer something different, he'd replied he had no appetite — for either my food, or what I was trying to convince him of. At once, I'd told him he needed to put his prejudice against the Catholics aside, and that his point of view was limited from his lack of experience. Without hesitation, he had then replied that his few years of experience had more value than my many spent choosing garments and arranging masques and dances. Did I, he had then asked tensely, forget how the Catholics had nearly brought about our destruction through their conspiracy in 1605? He had then taken a piece of bread and crumbled it, showing what he thought of the Spanish proposal. It would be preferable, he had said, for his sister to become a nun in some European convent, where they were at least sincere in their wrong beliefs, than to become a puppet of the Pope.

All had been said in a moderate tone, which had rendered the words even more difficult for me to accept. Understanding that arguing would be useless, I had said nothing. He had then apologised, while making it clear it wasn't for holding such opinions, only for expressing them so to me. Then, very neatly and precisely, he had begun to eat. But we'd finished the dinner in silence, and he'd departed, with cordial formality, not long after. Alone, I had sat at the table after the final dishes had been cleared away, looking at his empty chair. His mention of the conspiracy of 1605 had been especially disturbing. For the first time, I'd wondered if he'd been more affected by it, and permanently so, than James had been.

It had been several weeks until he'd visited me again, longer than usual, enough for me to decide that going forward, it would not be worth damaging the respectful way we dealt with each other by discussing politics. During that time, the possibility of the Spanish marriage ended for other reasons, and when we did see each other again, neither of us had even mentioned it.

Today, I hadn't been prepared for him to speak of Elizabeth, but I quickly reminded myself to be careful of what I said if it had to do with her marriage.

"Elizabeth?" I said, showing slight surprise. "What of her?"

"The king has decided which marriage proposal she should accept. You are aware of the choice, I assume?"

I wasn't, which annoyed me. But I would only have heard so officially, for James and I had grown so distant in past years, there would have been no opportunity for him to mention it casually. And if anyone in my household had heard it, they hadn't told me.

"I'm not," I answered, trying not to sound anxious.

Across from me, Henry suddenly looked out of place on the slender farthingale chair. They had been specially designed to accommodate the now fashionable wide circular-waisted dresses I had done much to make popular. But the chairs weren't suited to Henry, who had little interest in the courtiers' social events, although he could converse and dance better than any of them. A very stable chair would have been more comfortable for him, perhaps impressive for its carvings but not designed for easy and trite socialising in a crowded room.

"Are you uncomfortable on that chair?" I asked. "I can easily have another brought in for you."

"The chair is fine. If I'm uncomfortable at all, it's because I find you ignorant of so important a matter."

"I am usually the last to learn of anything these days," I said, in a tone suggesting I knew I shouldn't be.

"It's because you so seldom go out anywhere. Why do you sit here in this house watching life go by from your window?

You should be out and about, letting the people see their queen."

"I like it here. This is the first house I have ever felt is fully mine."

"My dear mother, every house in England and Scotland could be said to be yours. You are loved and respected everywhere." He said it in a very definite way, as though it were beyond doubt. Then he shifted position slightly on the chair, but still did not look settled on it. "Elizabeth is to marry Frederick, Count Palatine of the Rhine."

It was exactly what I had not wanted to hear. "The marriage is beneath her," I couldn't stop myself from saying. "This is more than disappointing. My daughter goes from being a princess of England and Scotland to little more than a German housewife."

"That is unfair," Henry answered quickly but evenly, having anticipated I would not be pleased with the choice. "Count Palatine is one of the finest men in Europe, despite not being a reigning monarch. He descends from Charlemagne and a line of counts going back seven hundred years. The Palatinate is a land of wealth and bounty, Heidelberg a city renowned for its sophistication. Strategically, it is central to everything that happens in Germany, and so Europe."

"They are of Reformed belief." I understood perfectly that this was central to the selection, although he hadn't said so.

"Yes — more similar to what we practised in Scotland than here. Count Palatine leads the German union to protect Reformed religion." A moment passed in awkward silence. Then, he went on, "There are significant benefits to this marriage, not only politically in giving us a new German ally, but for Elizabeth personally. The count is the same age as her, and reported to be handsome in appearance. He is scholarly, but not overly so, which suits since she is not, either. And there are excellent reports of his manner and disposition. He is said to be a very kind man. The king and I are in agreement that he should make Elizabeth an excellent husband, and that she would like life in the Palatinate."

"At least I can be thankful the two of you agree on something," I said pointedly.

"For now," he said, a little darkly. "Which brings me to the reason for my visit here today."

"Which is?"

"I want you to speak to the king about my own marriage."

"Is one decided?"

"Not yet, but there have been offers." He hesitated, then said, "I hope to rely on your assistance, should the king and I disagree."

I knew at once what that disagreement might be. "You do not want a Catholic wife."

"That should not come as a surprise to you."

"And the king might want a balance for this Reformed marriage for Elizabeth."

"Exactly."

"Has he spoken of it yet?" Although it was impossible to dissuade James from a course once he had set his mind to it, sometimes he would listen to differing points of view before deciding.

"No. But I am told he has recently met with the ambassador from Savoy. Which he did not, when last approached."

A few months ago, there had been proposals for marriages for both Henry and Elizabeth with the children of the Duke of Savoy, ruler of a group of valuable European lands between France and Italy, and a leader to be reckoned with. Despite his lack of a royal title, the proposals had pleased me, for the children's mother had been sister to the King of Spain. But James had decided against them, and negotiations had not proceeded. Now, though, the situation was different, with Elizabeth marrying into Reformed Germany. It was not difficult to see there might be wisdom in Henry's having a bride from a similar Catholic region.

"Would you really find the prospect of a Savoy marriage so impossible?" I asked delicately. "It wouldn't be quite the same as one would have been for Elizabeth. The bride would come to live here. She might even be convinced to change her religion."

His answer was quick: "Impossible. I want no part in any alliance with Spain, however indirect."

Although I knew the futility of trying to persuade him, I couldn't resist making one more attempt. "Henry, one of your father's most difficult traits is his inability to change his mind once he decides a matter is settled. Although I am loath to ever criticise him, I do believe at times some things would have had better results had he been able to do so. I mean personally, as well as for matters of state."

His face showed respectful attention, but with scepticism bordering on dismissal.. Nevertheless, I continued, "A few minutes ago I mentioned the discord between your father and me resulting from his removing you from my care when you were an infant. Because of his own disappointing childhood experience with his mother, he'd decided there was less chance of a repetition of history if his children were not in my care, and that they would be better off. I believed otherwise at the time, and I still do. It was only with the greatest of efforts that I overcame my objections. I tell you this now as a caution against the same behaviour. At times even our most deeply held beliefs should be reevaluated. For you, this may be one of them. I understand your intense dislike of the Catholics; everyone in this country knows it. But your sweeping rejection strikes me as not being in your best interest. Surely you understand that there are good and bad people who are Catholics, as there are Reformed? It is always the person that matters in the end. Would you not take the time to learn more of a proposed Catholic bride, perhaps even meeting in person first? Again, from my own experience, I know how important it is for a country for there to be personal harmony between a king and queen. So long as that exists, other problems of a political nature between them can be overcome. Even religion, which causes so much trouble today."

Abruptly, still seated, Henry slid the chair sideways, so he could look out of the window behind him. Outside, I saw in the distance that my women had gone across the lawn to the river, where they'd settled on the wall at the bank, overlooking it. Henry seemed to be looking at them, or perhaps at the passing boats on the river beyond.

Without turning to me, he said, "I would marry the worst-tempered crone in the world, no matter her parentage, so long as she were Reformed, before I would marry a Catholic."

The calmness of his tone startled me. "Henry," I began, but was stopped by his swiftly pushing the chair back around to face me.

"Your Majesty," he said, "a moment ago, you acknowledged that the entire country knows of my position regarding the Catholics. I would ask you to remember it. I have no doubt of the wisdom of your advice here today, and I would encourage any other man in this kingdom to take it. But I am not any other man in this kingdom. I am the Prince of Wales, set to follow my father as king. I do not have the luxury of behaving as anyone else would. For me it is different, and I must behave as such." He looked unseeingly into the room behind me. "Long, long ago, I had to set aside what I wished my life to be, in accepting the responsibilities of the position I had been born into. I have done so, and have clearly defined who I am as a prince for this nation, and what type of king is to follow. It is who I now am. Having put aside one sense of who I was as a child, I cannot now do so again. I have even come to like it. Certainly, I can see a future for myself in this kingdom, as I have now defined myself. That, Your Majesty, is as a Reformed prince. I have no wish to try to be something other than I am — once again. So please, Your Majesty —"

"Stop calling me that," I said, unable to hear him address me so again. "I am your mother."

"Mother, then. So as both mother and queen, I ask you to do what you can to prevent a marriage I do not want."

Beyond him, outside the window, the women were now spreading out in some game, the very picture of youthful cheerfulness. Henry should have been out there with them, instead of talking of politics and religion and how they would decide his marriage. Unknown to me, parts of him I'd thought minor had become more central to who he was.

"Yes, of course," I replied with sincerity, leaning forward. "But my ability to affect this is limited, especially since your father and I have become distant. What of the Secretary? James would be more inclined to listen to him. I'm sure he's already had a hand in arriving at this German marriage for Elizabeth. Unless he has changed in recent years, his opinions would certainly lean towards a Reformed marriage for you. And you and he have always got along. Can you not approach him? Or should I do so for you?"

"He is very ill, Mother," he answered. "He has gone to take the waters at Bath. But I'm told it is worse for him this time."

It was shocking news. For more than a year the Secretary's health had been poor, but there'd been signs of recovery, and I had never yet imagined that we would be without him. His wisdom would be irreplaceable. "The poor man," I said, trying to hold back the returning panic. "We must pray for him."

"Indeed. For many reasons, including this. But we cannot be so unkind as to ask his assistance unless he at least somewhat recovers and returns here. There's no question that he could help us, though. Your assumption that he would favour a Reformed marriage is correct. We have even discussed it, and he was clear he would prefer a German or Scandinavian match, or English, or even Scottish. He had once felt an English bride would be best, because of my Scottish birth. But that necessity has faded. The English now view us as their own."

I wanted to reply that he had me to thank for it, for if I'd had more sons in England they might now be viewed as more fitting for the throne than him. But, outside of initial conversations with my brother and the Secretary, I had never told anyone that it had been the main reason why I'd stopped having children.

"I haven't visited your father for a while," I said agreeably. "It may be time for me to do so. While there, I can tell him I would like to see you marry a bride of your own choice. That way, there's more chance of a meaningful response from him, than if I tried to speak of the politics of a German or Scandinavian marriage. He knows I do not have enough understanding of diplomacy to offer an opinion worth listening to. He may be less dismissive if I present it as a family matter."

Henry visibly relaxed, leaning back on the chair. "Thank you, Mother," he said simply.

"Remember your poor old mother," I said meaningfully, with a touch of self-pity, "when you are king and I am fading away, forgotten by all."

"Why do you say things like that? You should not even suggest it might happen."

I seldom made such remarks, although it was a subject often in my thoughts. For years, the expectation that my future security would depend on Henry more than James had been part of many of my decisions. "I am already forgotten. Only the members of my own household pay me any respect. Few members of the court or the nobility visit me here. I barely ever see my own husband or children." I pretended to wipe away a tear. "And now, you tell me my only daughter is to move far away."

From a pocket he withdrew a handkerchief, its perfect whiteness an unexpectedly stark contrast to his black attire. "For your tears, mother," he said evenly as he reached forward to hand it to me. "It is nonsense to think yourself ignored. As I said before, you should be out and about more."

"I told you, I like it here." The present need to walk a line between James as the current king and Henry as the future one existed for me as much as everyone else. In some ways it accounted for my withdrawal from much of court life, for it avoided the possibility of my being placed in difficult positions. Living my own life at Denmark House was more comfortable for me. But it also meant I missed much information, and when I had the opportunity to gather it, I took it. "Now, tell me what you know of this German marriage for Elizabeth. Has she been told yet?"

"Yes."

"Is she agreeable?"

"Very much so. Early on, miniature portraits were exchanged. She and Count Palatine were both pleased with what they saw. All that remains is to work out satisfactory marriage terms, which should take a few months. Then, the count is to come here in autumn for the wedding."

"It would be better for them to meet in person while there is still time for a change, should either find a great difference between life and the portraits. You are aware of the dislike King Henry took to his German bride, Anne of Cleves, upon seeing her? Divorce soon followed."

"Yes, I have heard tell of it."

"It mattered nothing that a portrait had been sent in advance. Hopefully, there won't be any repetition of that for Elizabeth when she sees him. As for Count Palatine, he can only be even more taken with her beauty when he sees her. Certainly, he'll want to whisk her away to Germany."

Henry smiled a little sadly. "I am going to miss her. There are so few here who have any understanding of what it has been like for one in my position. She and I shared much of the same experience, coming here from Scotland. We have spoken of how strange it was to be stared at when we arrived, not only by the crowds, but even the nobility."

"Royal children were new to them. Yes, everyone was very excited about you, and wanted to see you."

"It made us feel we were so very different from other children, so much more important, and that a great many things depended on us." His smile became polite. "And they do. So now, we must both be especially careful in choosing who we marry. Please, do what you can to help me."

Once again, I told him I would. He then stood and took the chair back to the same place he had taken it from. After setting it down, he hesitated, then moved it ever so slightly, angling it in a certain way against the wall. "Back in its place," he said, more to himself than me.

I stood and accompanied him to the door. "You can expect to hear from me within a week about this," I told him. "My visit should be in the next few days. I only need to compose my thoughts first."

When he was gone, I went back to the windows. The women were all sitting on the river wall. They would be disappointed that they'd had no chance to see Henry before he'd left. But they would all be pleased to hear that in a few days, they would be accompanying me to Whitehall Palace.

13

The next morning, I sent a message to James that I had a matter to discuss with him, and wanted to know when would be best for me to come to Whitehall. Within hours a reply came that the following day would be convenient, unless I intended to remain the night, in which case it would take longer to have my rooms prepared.

"Tell them tomorrow is fine," I said to Anna. "I don't want to stay there any longer than I have to. I suppose I'll have to dine with the court in the banquet hall, but right after that we'll come back here."

"Shall we go by river, or along the Strand? You haven't been riding in a while, and it might be nice to let the people in the streets see you."

"By river. If it rains, we can have a closed barge."

But the weather turned out fine, and a little after midmorning we boarded the small fleet of river barges with the royal insignia. The soft breeze and occasional white clouds drifting across the blue sky were calming, and I knew the barges had been a much better choice for the trip than riding through the streets full of staring citizens, eager to see me smile and wave at them from my horse. Today it would have been difficult, for a by now familiar anxiety had taken hold of me as I anticipated seeing James. I knew I should never feel so about visiting my husband of so many years, but each time I'd seen him in recent years, he had seemed more different. There had been recognisable strands of his old self, but when I'd reached for familiar touchstones in how he thought and felt, I'd found them vanished. Had I been with him daily, it might have been otherwise, but by then we'd been settled into our separate routines, and it had felt too late to go back.

Mary's death had briefly made me consider approaching him about resuming our life as husband and wife, and possibly having more children. But I had chosen not to, because of the threat it could present to Henry's succession. We had continued as we were, the gulf between us widening as the years had passed. It had been something I'd calmly accepted as part of the inevitable changes encountered in life. But whenever I'd needed to visit him, I'd found myself uncomfortable and unsure as the meeting approached. This time was no different, and I became more and more apprehensive as the barge drew closer to the palace.

At the Water Gate, he was waiting with some courtiers on the steps, behind the porters there to assist me and the women from our barges. The courtesy was unexpected and encouraging, for there was no protocol for how I should be received on an informal visit, and I'd thought to be met only by the usual palace officials. Anyone could have easily identified him as the king among the gentlemen, his clothing new and stylish, his short gold and brown coat and beige tunic perfectly fitted. But at almost forty-six, he looked his age, if not older, and although his beard and moustache were still the same very light brown, his hair would be grey when he removed his plumed hat. As the porters helped me from the barge and he came down the few steps to take my hand, I saw something not easily definable about his face that also spoke of his having aged. His eyelids were still nearly half closed in their usual way, but when he looked directly at me, his blue eyes seemed more subdued than I'd ever seen them before.

"Anne," he said smoothly, as everyone on the steps bowed, while I curtsied to him, still holding his hand.

I'd rehearsed a pleasant greeting but suddenly found I couldn't remember it. "James," was all I could say instead.

"Looking quite your usual beautiful self," he said flatteringly. "Life at Denmark House agrees with you." He smiled in the slight way he always had, giving me immediate hope that he was still unchanged enough for me to be comfortable with. He extended his arm for me to place my hand on, and I did so. Side by side, we went into the palace, our retinues trailing behind us.

One of the large rooms of my suite had been opened and hastily prepared, and he left me at its door, asking me to come to his reception room in half an hour's time. Inside was a table with wine and beer, and light foods we might want to fortify ourselves with after the little trip on the river. There were also servants waiting to assist if my attire or any of the women's needed adjustment. The hospitality was an additional good sign, showing concern for my comfort. But as I looked around the large, nicely decorated room, I felt a stranger in it, although I had once used it often and could still call it my own. Those satisfying years at Whitehall after we had arrived from Scotland were long gone.

Anna helped me remove my cloak, and the other women tidied my hair with combs. "Enough," I said. "My husband knows what I look like. A stray lock of hair won't trouble him." Several of them laughed, and I felt more relaxed. When one brought me a cup of wine, I drank it. Then, Anna came forward with the jewellery I'd chosen, too valuable to have worn during the busy and sometimes chaotic barge trip. As I put on the diamond and emerald rings, broaches and necklace, it felt like donning armour, as if I were about to do battle with James. Quickly, I dismissed the thought, which was all the more nonsensical because the jewels had been given to me by him.

The door opened, and the Countess of Bedford was announced as she strode into the room. The sight of my old friend was immediately reassuring and somehow gave me confidence.

"I didn't know you were expected," she said after her obligatory curtsey. "I've been here at court with my husband for more than a week."

I shooed the women away and walked with her to a window, so we could talk privately in the short time before I saw James. "Henry wants me to help him avoid a Catholic marriage. He fears James might now choose one to balance Elizabeth's forthcoming marriage. You know that it is decided?"

"Yes. Are you agreeable to it?"

"My opinion was not sought. Not by her or anyone." I allowed only a hint of resentment in the way I said it. "But now I am needed — by Henry. As his mother, I must do what I can."

Her dark eyes grew thoughtful. She was skilled politically, and had been of great help to her husband, a leading Reformer, both directly as his confidante, and indirectly through patronage of artists and writers. Then, she said, "What I have heard is that the king is undecided about which bride to choose for Henry. But what he found favourable about the German marriage for Elizabeth is its unlikelihood of leading to England's involvement in foreign wars as an ally. He may very well apply the same thinking to the match for Henry, which would point to a Reformed choice, domestic or foreign. So, it might not be a difficult task you have today."

This new information was valuable. I took her hand and squeezed it. "I have so few friends," I said gratefully. She placed her other hand over mine. As she did, her many rings became visible. Despite her religion, she loved jewellery and fine clothing nearly as much as I did, and avoided the traditional Reformed simplicity in attire. Her dress today, wide with a farthingale, was of expensive grey satin, trimmed with lace and silver needlework.

She then told me that she knew Elizabeth had seen Count Palatine's portrait and responded favourably. Often she heard news regarding her, for her father was Elizabeth's guardian, overseeing her household at Coombe Abbey. "But, Your Majesty, if you have not spoken with her directly about her marriage, you must. Nothing can replace what you have to tell her, as her mother. Even if you have reservations, you should speak of them. Tell the king today you intend to visit her. I would like nothing more than to accompany you. Along the way we can make plans for the wedding celebrations. Of course, there must be a masque."

One of my women approached, saying the king had sent a message to say he was ready to see me. As I left, the countess said quietly, "Don't forget, Henry is not your only child. Your daughter has need of you also. And so does your other son."

"Thank you, my friend. You must sit beside the king and I at dinner today."

Her reminder about Charles lingered with me as I made my way to James's rooms. He and Henry, at least, had developed a strong family bond, unlike the rest of us. It had been an excellent decision to place him in Henry's household, under his supervision. But because of it, Charles had receded even further from my thoughts than before. His previous guardians, the Careys, had been diligent in reporting even the most routine matters, demonstrating their attentiveness. But Henry oversaw his brother's education and behaviour without seeking oversight from us. The occasions when I did see Charles gave me no cause for concern, and neither did the indirect reports I received from his tutors and others in the St James's Palace household. James had no complaints either, and we had been content to allow Henry nearly complete independence in his decisions. But when he married, there would need to be a change. The young couple would need their own household during the early years when they'd be coming to know each other, and Charles's presence would be a distraction. The countess's suggestion that I pay more attention to him might be timely, so I could determine what would be best for him next. I might mention it to James today, along with my visit to Elizabeth.

Since my rooms at Whitehall were not fully open, I hadn't been able to use the private connection to James's suite, and instead had to pass through his main reception room, where his courtiers and visitors were gathered. As the footmen opened its large double doors, I saw that it was full to overflowing, as it had always been in any of our palaces, even back in Scotland. All conversation stopped as I entered, the crowd dividing and sweeping back in two colourful waves to allow me a path through to the inner rooms. On both sides everyone bowed or curtsied, and the words "Your Majesty" passed along as I went by. I scanned for friends and recognisable faces, but was surprised by how few I found. Most of the courtiers looked younger than I had ever seen. I wondered if James had chosen to surround himself with them as a way of contending with his own advancing years. I had done something similar at Denmark House; my women were mostly youthful and could always be relied upon to provide cheer even on the dreariest of days.

At the entrance to the inner rooms, my attendants fell back and merged with the crowd, and I proceeded in alone. Fortunately, the footman brought me to one of the parlours, rather than James's library, which I had years ago come to dislike. The overcrowded shelves and cabinets full of books and papers had always been a reminder that his intellectual abilities surpassed mine, and that he was a scholar while I was not.

The parlour door opened, showing two greyhounds right inside, as though waiting to greet me. "Dogs, away," James said from within, and the footman beckoned them past me. As they went by, both looked at me with mild interest. There had been a time when I had known all of James's dogs. But these, I did not.

James came forward, now wearing a short brown velvet jacket. His hat was absent, so I could see that his hair was indeed much streaked with grey. He led me to a pair of chairs facing each other before a fireplace in which there was a small fire beneath the marble mantle. The chairs were armless and didn't match the other furniture in the room, which consisted of heavier wooden pieces, with several large cabinets. It was likely they contained valuable objects, small works of art or curiosities, but suddenly I was disturbed by not knowing what they were. As I sat down, I consoled myself that at least an effort had been made to ensure my comfort with chairs appropriate for the wideness of my dress. No doubt that if I lived at Whitehall, or spent more time there, it would be furnished more to suit me.

"Wine?" James asked.

"No, thank you."

He sat down on the other chair, his movements smoother than when he'd been younger, if slower and more deliberate.

He folded his hands together and asked in an accommodating tone, "And so, what did you wish to see me about today?"

"Our children's marriages. I understand you have decided Elizabeth should marry Count Palatine."

"Yes."

I waited for him to say more, but he didn't. I had expected he might offer some excuse for not having told me already, but he simply sat with his hands together, looking at me with a pleasant expression on his face. Apparently, it had not occurred to him that I might be offended he had not considered my opinion worthwhile enough to have sought beforehand, or that he had not even told me of the decision afterward.

An uneasy anger began to form within me, but it would not serve my purpose to start arguing. Trying my best not to sound critical or disapproving, I said, "I learned of it a few days ago, from Henry."

I had some final hope that my saying so might prompt him to understand how I felt, and that he would at least offer an apology. Instead, he merely said, "Henry." It was impossible to tell whether he was surprised by his having told me.

"Yes. He is, of course, very pleased with the decision."

"Yes," he replied, again in smooth but empty way that told me nothing.

I looked away from him, trying to steady myself. His lack of response was confusing, leaving me at a loss as to how to proceed. I had expected to find him changed, but this time, I wasn't finding anything at all.

There was nothing to do but explain directly why I had come. "Henry is very concerned that you might decide he should marry a Catholic bride, which he would not want. He has asked me to speak to you on his behalf. Although I might myself prefer that for him, I must put his future contentment and peace of mind first. I am here today to ask you to honour his wishes. Surely there are enough available choices in northern Europe, or here at home, for you to find a Reformed bride who would be to England's benefit."

"I see," he said.

This time, there had been curtness in the brevity of his response, telling me he hadn't liked some aspect of what I'd said. But I didn't know if it was Henry's objection to a Catholic bride, or his having spoken to me of it, or my having taken his side in the matter. It was time to appeal to his emotions.

"Surely, James, you'd agree the marriage has a greater chance of success if it is harmonious. It's what we both want, isn't it? Nothing is ever certain in marriage. But why not do what we can to create the best possible chances of an amicable match?"

"You should not interfere in this," James said with an abruptness that was surprising even after the curtness he'd already displayed.

"Interfere?" I could barely restrain my indignation. "We are speaking of my son!"

His response was quick: "Who is to be king." He looked tense. "He still has much to learn of his responsibilities."

"He is the very model of a prince!"

He seemed about to stand, and I thought he might leave the room, so unused was he to anyone disagreeing with him. But he stayed seated and said, "Henry has strange ideas, even for a very young man. Thus far, he seems incapable of viewing the world with objectivity. His religious views are those of a bigot of the worst kind."

I was about to strongly disagree, but stopped. Henry kept so much to himself that I knew little of what he believed, or how he thought about the world. And, as much as I would have liked to, I couldn't disagree about his attitude towards religion.

James continued, "The strangeness I expect he can grow out of, as he becomes increasingly involved in the affairs of the state. He'll come to see the need for practicality and accurate assessment of what is possible, and what is not. But I worry most about the depth of his intolerance of the Catholics. To that end, I have thought a Catholic bride could teach him."

"You have been no supporter of Catholics," I couldn't stop myself from saying. "You hold him to a standard you do not adhere to yourself! It is I who have sought a more moderate attitude towards them."

"No. I have always wanted an easier balance with them, and tolerance. Although circumstances and their own foolish actions have made it impossible, I still have hopes for the future, not only here, but in all of Europe. Henry could play a significant role in accomplishing it."

"That is your dream, not his."

He pulled lightly at the sleeve of his jacket, a sign of his agitation. Out of everything I'd said, my last remark had made an impression. He said, "I believe in time he may feel differently. There is much to be considered here, of international concern. Although my mind is not made up yet, I do feel our daughter's marriage should be balanced with a Catholic one. Personal feelings cannot come into play in this decision."

"When have they not for us?" I asked, not yet ready to accept it. "It can be easy for those in our positions to delude ourselves, when so few dare to challenge our choices."

"I strive always for objectivity," he said quietly, but again, he pulled at his sleeve.

"And I for what is best for our family."

"You delude yourself. For years you have wanted Spanish marriages for our children, not for their betterment, but to aggrandise your own prestige. Of the two of us, it is you who has been unable to free yourself of personal feelings in your decisions."

I could scarcely believe what he had said. My face must have shown how startled I was, for his manner changed at once.

"Dearest Anne," he said nicely, "let us not quarrel and be unpleasant with each other. I am sure we both want what is best for our children. I understand your concern, and it shall be taken into account when I make my decision. But that may be some time yet. First, the terms for the German marriage must be successfully negotiated. Should they not be, circumstances would be different."

I recognised that he was trying to soothe my feelings, retreating from what he'd said. But I also understood my opinion would still count for nothing.

He stood up and came to me, extending his hand. "Come, let us now join the others, perhaps in a walk through the garden before we go in to dine. The courtiers here have so few opportunities to see you — I'm sure they are delighted by the visit. Let them see us together in complete accord."

Although I didn't want to, I took his hand and allowed him to lead me to the door. We were almost there when I asked, "How has the Secretary advised you in this?"

I half expected him to be evasive, but he answered directly, "He favours Reformed marriages for both Elizabeth and Henry. That is to be expected, considering his dislike of the Spanish. But it may be time for the country to put that animosity behind us. Besides, he won't be with us much longer. He's been quite ill for some time, you know. I don't expect him to live to see either marriage. And thus, it is going to be for me alone to contend with their consequences, whatever they may be."

The Secretary's loss would deprive him of one of the few people whose opinion he valued and relied upon, even if he did so with a show of near indifference and an air of patronising tolerance that his pride demanded. Without Cecil, the years ahead were going to be even more difficult for James when it came to seeing differing points of view. He would use youth as an excuse to dismiss Henry's views, and lack of experience to ignore mine.

My only hope was that Cecil might still recover and be able to convince James to do as Henry wanted. "The poor man," I said sympathetically. "Is he so badly off? I know he's gone to Bath for treatment."

"I don't expect him to return," James said with finality. Somehow, I knew I wouldn't be able to seek Cecil's help ever again.

The door opened and we went back to the crowded reception room I'd passed through earlier. Everyone bowed or curtsied, and when someone called out, "God save King James and Queen Anne!" it was repeated by all, in one resounding cheer. We were doing exactly what James had wanted, presenting a picture of domestic unity. But as I smiled and graciously acknowledged all who pressed forward to offer good wishes, I could think only about how poorly the conversation with him had gone. Despite my lack of competence in politics and governance, in family matters, James should have had more respect for my opinions. His comment that I had been selfish in my motives had been one of the unkindest things he'd ever said to me, intentionally belittling. As I now gave trite and silly replies to the courtiers' witty quips and observations, I felt empty. For James, nothing I did or said made any difference any longer. Despite the show of attention and respect he was giving me, I was little more than a character in a masque after it was over.

A feeble thought came that I shouldn't accept it, that I should try again to make him understand the worthiness of what I had to say. It wasn't too late, and I could easily draw him aside into a private conversation. But sudden anxiety clawed at me. More than anything, I wanted to be back at Denmark House, or anywhere other than Whitehall Palace.

"Shall we go into the garden now?" James asked, already leading me in the direction of the stairs down to it, the courtiers trailing behind us like children in a game.

Outside the air was cooler despite the brilliant midday sunshine, comfortable to walk in since the garden was enclosed on four sides and sheltered from the Thames breezes. I felt easier, the anxiety receding, but not the sense of loss, of being unable to achieve what I'd wanted. Then, from the opposite direction on the path, the Countess of Bedford approached. A different type of path seemed to open before me, an indirect way around James's stubbornness.

"The countess and I want to visit Elizabeth," I told him as she reached us. "We spoke of it earlier before I came in to see you."

"Walk with us, countess," he said welcomingly. "So, the queen tells me the two of you wish to visit Elizabeth?"

"It was I who suggested it, Your Majesty. A daughter needs her mother's company at such an important time in her life."

"Then by all means you must go. I can think of few nicer pastimes than a trip to Coombe Abbey in this beautiful spring weather."

"Sooner rather than later," I said. "While this stretch of fine weather continues."

And as we walked on further, I wondered if there might be a portrait of the son of the Duke of Savoy in London, and if I could get it before going to Coombe Abbey.

That evening after supper back at Denmark House, when my women asked if I would prefer to have musical entertainment or to play cards, I told them I wanted to see my jewellery collection. It was not an unfamiliar request for them, and they complied easily. Case after case was brought out from the care of a steward and unlocked and opened, the contents removed and placed beneath the two candelabras on the white silk-covered table before me. Anna, inventory in hand, hovered closely, checking each item as it emerged, diamonds, pearls, rubies and emeralds set in gold and silver. Some, I remembered how I'd obtained, by gift or purchase, although there were so many I often did not.

Contentment and gratification came over me almost immediately. In a short amount of time, the dissatisfied mood that had been with me since leaving Whitehall that afternoon was gone.

14

Elizabeth emerged exuberantly, with her attendants, from the entrance of Coombe Abbey as our line of coaches and accompanying guards arrived. Always beautiful, she looked even more so now that she was full of hopes and expectations. Her long hair, thick and curling, had darkened to an attractive reddish light brown, and was unfixed and flowing about her shoulders in a very natural way. In her pale pink dress, it seemed as though spring itself rushed forward with her to embrace me as I stepped out of the coach. Somehow, despite the little time we were ever together, a bond had been maintained between us, and I returned her embrace with equal affection.

She linked her arm through mine, briefly looking back to greet the Countess of Bedford who'd been in the coach with me, and led me towards the mansion's entrance as the rest of my entourage arrived. Her little group of attendants, all of a similar age and radiating the same enthusiasm for life, curtsied as we passed. They seemed more animated than any of the women at Whitehall or Denmark House ever did. Behind us, the countess must have noticed it also, and when she remarked good-naturedly that she was already feeling rather matronly among them, there was laughter and reassurances of the beauty of both of us. I laughed too, despite knowing full well my days of youth were long gone. Each year it took more and more effort to maintain the image of the beautiful queen the people wanted.

Inside we were greeted by the countess's parents, Lord and Lady Harrington, Elizabeth's guardians. Now elderly, they had, when James first arrived in England, held a magnificent reception at one of their estates to welcome him. Their reward had been the prestige of becoming the princess's guardians, which they had carried out successfully at Coombe Abbey for nine years. Fortunately, Lord Harrington was a man of great wealth, for rumours were that the cost of maintaining Elizabeth's household always exceeded his allowance from James and Parliament, and he provided the extra money himself.

I had been there only once, briefly when Elizabeth had moved in. Near Coventry, it was in the centre of the country and our present trip had required an overnight stay along the way at a house that had not been all that comfortable. Although the weather had continued fine and the early May countryside had been lovely, and the countess had been an excellent companion, the trip had been tiring. In stark contrast to Elizabeth's attendants, my own looked rumpled and irritable, having spent the previous night in tents. But Lord and Lady Harrington had anticipated we might arrive in such condition, and immediately had us shown to the rooms prepared for us.

The house's origin as an abbey was still apparent in the Gothic details, but it had been converted into a modern building very successfully, with spacious rooms with many large fireplaces and windows. My bedroom suite was luxuriously appointed with fine panelling, ribbed plaster ceilings, tapestries of mythological scenes and heavily carved furniture, including canopied oak beds with velvet covers and pillows. Although it was only late afternoon, we all retired immediately, with Lady Harrington telling us supper would be brought to our rooms. As we were to stay for several days, there was no need to begin the visit until morning. Elizabeth, though, remained in my rooms with me for a while, expertly directing the servants in unpacking and arranging my belongings. "I'd like nothing better than to stay longer," she said when satisfied everything was in order. "But I must see that the countess and your women are all settled in as well." Leaving me to the care of Anna, she went out.

"She takes responsibility," Anna said admiringly, when we were alone. "A great queen she would make for a country."

"A great waste it would be for her to become merely Goodwife Palatine. And perhaps she won't."

Anna said nothing, but I knew she understood. With effort, it had been she who had obtained for me from the Savoyard ambassador the miniature portrait of the duke's son, which I had brought with me. It had been painted when the unsuccessful double Savoyard marriage for Henry and Elizabeth had been proposed. With it the ambassador had sent a message that he also had one of the duke's daughter, who had been and might still be considered for Henry, should I wish to see it. Nothing would have pleased me more, but I now needed to do what I could to help Henry achieve a marriage he wanted.

I rested a while and then ate with surprising appetite the sumptuous supper the Harringtons had sent to me. Afterward, before going to bed, I went to one of the windows to look out over the three-sided courtyard we'd passed through when arriving. It had the look of a monastic cloister, as though from the original building. It was strange to think that monks had lived in the house for so many years.

There was a knock at the door to the outer room, and Anna opened it and spoke with a servant on the other side. Lord Harrington, she then told me, was there to see I had everything

I needed. As I was still sufficiently dressed for visitors, I asked him to be shown in.

An affable-looking older man, he had a mane of thick white hair that only slightly receded on each side of his forehead, and a face mostly without the creases of age. His clothing was of the simpler and less elaborate style of the Puritans, although not severely so, and his manner was clear and direct, without affectation, as was his speech. There was no pretentiousness about him, and I was sure, by similarity with others he reminded me of, that his main ambition in life had been to be useful and purposeful. Many of those same qualities had been inherited by his daughter, and were some of the reasons I so valued her friendship.

"You have come at the right moment," I told him after he bowed. "I do want something — knowledge. I was thinking of the time when the house was an abbey. What can you tell me of it?" I sat down in a carved chair large enough to be a throne.

As I'd thought he might be, he was proud of the house and was delighted to share its history with me. "The monastery was founded in the twelfth century by the Cistercian monks," he explained. "It was dedicated to Mary, as the Blessed Mother. They were devout, hardworking men, following the rules of Benedict, a saint, as the Catholics call him. They led a simple, austere life in the service of God. Their pursuits were agrarian, not intellectual. They worked the land with success and the monastery flourished. It became renowned for its gifts to the poor each week, from the bounty of the land."

He stopped, as though carefully reminding himself of the current very different attitude towards Catholics in our country. Although Reformed, it was clear he admired the monks of old, for their work and charity. To set him at ease, I said, "There was much reason to respect the monks in those days. They were good men in those times, which were very different from today. And I have never found insult or harm in the veneration of Mary as the mother of Jesus, though I regard it as without meaning."

"We know better today, Your Majesty," he said, smiling gently. "My daughter, who studies the classics, would tell you there were worthy pagans also, in the times before Jesus. But those are theological matters beyond the comprehension of an old man like me."

"And me, I'm afraid," I replied, being careful myself. "Let us speak of what we understand. Tell me more of the house. I assume it was taken from the monks by King Henry when he broke from Rome?"

"Yes, during the dissolution. All of the monasteries and convents, no matter which order, became the property of the state. Henry sold them to the nobles, who were eager to own them. Including, I must say, some who resisted his religious changes and still professed loyalty to the Church of Rome. That didn't prevent them from making a good profit at their Church's expense."

His remark told me that no matter how benevolently he viewed the monks who had once worked in the abbey, he was still Reformed, with a dislike of the Catholics. If he'd had any say, he would have approved of the marriage with Count Palatine that James had chosen for Elizabeth. I would find no ally in him in trying to turn her towards a match with the son of the Duke of Savoy instead.

Behind me, I heard Anna exhale quickly in disapproval. Diplomatically, I said, "Unfortunately, there are always such people when money is involved, Catholic and Reformed alike. Such is human nature. Those who are wise in authority understand it. I heard that when Henry's daughter Mary became queen and restored Catholicism, she decided not to attempt to take back the property and return it to the Roman Church." Again, we had drifted into a discussion of religion that I wanted to avoid. But it was difficult not to, given how connected to the building it had been. "So, the new owners changed the church buildings into residences, then," I said, redirecting our conversation more specifically to the house.

"Mostly, yes. They tore down the churches and used the stone to build new mansions, or to expand and alter the existing buildings. That is what they did here. The open south side of the courtyard where you entered was where the church stood, providing the fourth wall of the cloisters."

"I thought it might be. Not just from the details — there's something in the feeling of the rooms."

His face showed concern. "Are you uncomfortable, Your Majesty? I can easily accommodate you elsewhere in the house."

"No, not at all. I find it rather charming. Tell me, was it you who changed it over to a private home?"

"It was started before me. After the king took it, there were different owners for forty years before I bought it in the 1580s. By then, the church was long gone, and a house had been fashioned around the remaining three sides of the cloisters. But it wasn't a very good or comfortable one. Most efforts had been put into maintaining the farmland, with the property used more for profit than a residence. I felt differently. The first time I came here, I saw the potential for a lovely house."

"Which you have certainly brought about," I said admiringly. "My daughter has been living in a charming setting. I couldn't be more pleased."

"Thank you for saying so, Your Majesty. It is very gracious of you to do so."

"Although I still wish I'd been able to raise her myself," I surprised myself by suddenly saying.

Lord Harrington looked as confused by what I'd said as I was. I had no idea what had prompted me to say it, or why I then continued, "I'd wanted to raise all of my children by myself. It was what we did in Denmark. But the king felt differently. I initially resisted, when our firstborn, Henry, was taken away from me. It was a cause of great trouble between the king and me. But finally, I saw it was useless for me to continue the struggle. When Elizabeth and our other children were then born, I simply accepted it as inevitable. But it does seem to have turned out well for Elizabeth, after all."

He lowered his head and said, "My wife and I have done our best."

He now no longer looked concerned or confused, but outright disturbed. Never should I have voiced such matters to him. At once, I said, "Yes, of course you have, and your best has been excellent. I can't thank you enough."

He relaxed and appeared at ease again. I heard Anna cough, delicately and politely, a subtle suggestion that I end the visit. "Thank you, Lord Harrington, for having taken this time to talk with me, when you must be busy with so many guests in your home. Your kindness is appreciated." He bowed and, a little awkwardly for an older man and one unused to it, walked backwards from the room.

"I said too much to him," I then told Anna. "I don't know why I should choose to speak of such things at this time."

"It's a new place, and a different type of house than you're used to. It has an effect."

I remained seated on the large, throne-like chair, still wondering why I had spoken as I had. Gradually, my attention was drawn to the tapestries covering most of two walls of the room. They depicted figures in ancient dress that was clearly different from that of biblical characters. But I didn't know who they were, as I would have with any Bible scene, or what stories they represented. They were part of the ancient religion that had faded after the start of Christianity, and finally vanished. From my education I knew something of it, of many gods and goddesses who'd clashed and bickered. The ancient people who had worshipped them had also fought each other, in wars like the one for Troy, for power and wealth and even love. But they had never struggled with each other over religion.

"There was much truth about human nature in the tales of the world before Christianity, although fantastical," I said musingly to Anna. "It makes one wonder if our struggles with religion today conceal other motives beneath. And how the world would be now, had that religion of old continued."

This time, I heard no delicate cough from her, but a sharp intake of breath. "Thank God for showing us the way, through the chosen people of old, and his own divine son," she replied severely.

Once again, I knew I had said too much. It was strange that I did so, given my understanding of the need to always be cautious in even my most casual remarks. Perhaps my indiscretion was caused by the feeling of the monastery lingering about the house, the monks having lived here at a more peaceful time, before the Christian schisms that had torn apart Europe.

I asked Anna to bring me the little portrait of the son of the Duke of Savoy. "I need to think on how best to present it to Elizabeth. I certainly can't be saying irrelevant things like I've been doing today."

It was in a small leather-covered case with a padded interior of soft blue velvet. The gold-framed portrait, a watercolour miniature on vellum the size of a playing card, showed a young man with a handsome, strong face, dark eyes, thick, curling black hair and a moustache. "Victor Amadeus," I said aloud. The name suited the face, which held an expression both dashing and romantic. Elizabeth would surely respond favourably to it. The best strategy might be for me to show it to her first, without saying who it was. Then, after she knew, I would tell her of the many excellent things I'd heard about him, and the fine future she would be able to look forward to as his wife. Feeling more certain of my course now, I closed the case and gave it back to Anna. "Have this readily available for me tomorrow," I told her. "I intend to show it to my daughter the first opportunity I get."

15

I slept well and rose at dawn. My attendants and I joined Elizabeth and hers for prayers in the chapel. The compact room, devoid of religious décor, was crowded to overflowing with both of our retinues along with the Harringtons' household, and I supposed Lord Harrington for the first time probably missed the original monastery's much larger church. We then went to breakfast in the more commodious banquet hall, where Elizabeth and I sat side by side on the dais, flanked by Lord and Lady Harrington. Finishing, Elizabeth accompanied me back to my rooms. "I am so eager to visit with you," she told me on the way. "Usually, this time is reserved for study. First, I read the Bible, then converse with the chaplain about it. Then, I have my French and Italian lessons. I've become quite proficient at them, both in writing and conversation. I'm learning German too now, and have a tutor especially for it, but I'm not nearly as good at that yet. I'm going to need much practice to be able to master some of it by the time Count Palatine arrives here. It's a sign of respect for me to greet him in his own language."

Evasively, I asked if she had music lessons as well. "Yes," she replied, "but not in the morning. I like to ride or at least walk outside before the midday meal. The weather is so fine, I hope you can join me when I do later."

"I don't ride nearly as much as I used to, but today I think I would like to. But let us have a talk first."

We arrived at my rooms, where we dismissed our attendants, leaving them to their own company. The night's rest had been an excellent restorative for my women, and their sour moods of the previous day had been thrown off. They mingled cheerfully with Elizabeth's women, as though they were all old friends. Anna left too, handing me the portrait of Victor Amadeus on her way out.

Elizabeth noticed, and as soon as we were alone, asked with mild curiosity, "And what have you there?"

"Something I've brought to show you. A gift, in a way."

Intrigued, her blue eyes widened questioningly. "A portrait?" she asked as she came to where I stood in the centre of the room and took it.

"Yes."

"Of whom?"

"Open it."

She had likely expected someone in our family, for she looked surprised when she saw a face she didn't recognise. But I was delighted to see her genuine interest, which she trusted me enough to display freely. I waited while her gaze remained fixed on the portrait, long enough for me to tell it appealed to her. Then her eyes met mine with a frank, open look as she asked, "Who is this very handsome man?"

"Victor Amadeus. The son of the Duke of Savoy."

Startled, she blinked. An instant later, it was as though a curtain descended between us, so completely did her expression change. The open look in her eyes vanished, replaced by one of polite reserve. She actually took a step back from me.

Quickly, I said, "He would be honoured to become your husband."

"I'm betrothed," she replied, with finality.

"Not yet. There is time to change your mind, should you want to."

The leather case of the portrait made a snapping sound as she closed it, then handed it back to me. "I've already agreed to marry Count Palatine. I've said so not only to him, but to my father the king, and my brother the prince. The marriage pleases all of them. I cannot make a change now, even if I wanted to. Which I don't."

She held the portrait towards me urgently, but I refused to accept it.

"My dear daughter, please, hear me out. I know this is a surprise for you. But I have only your best interests in mind." Self-reproachfully, I remembered my true motivation was to help Henry, not her. But under any circumstances I would have preferred the Savoian marriage to the German one. There was nothing wrong with my now trying to bring it about. "Please, listen to my thoughts. I am your mother, and it is only right that you take them into account for something as important as your marriage." Abruptly, without forethought, I added, "Although I am at a loss as to why they have not yet been sought. Neither by your father, nor your brother, nor you."

The words sounded very bitter, even to me. Distress and confusion now replaced the polite look on her face, but at least she did not retreat further behind a mask of caution and was still allowing me to see what she truly felt. Although what I had just said had been manipulative, it had been successful. But seeing her so disturbed me deeply. Immediately, I decided that if she started to cry, I would proceed no further.

Still holding the portrait, her eyes fluttered closed, and for a moment she remained still. When she opened them, her gaze was fixed directly on my face. "Does the king know you are speaking to me of this?"

"Not exactly, no. But he approved this visit. He must know I intend to discuss marriage."

"Your Majesty my mother, he would not be pleased by it."

"I know. But it is important enough for me to do so anyway. I believe you would find little joy in becoming Goodwife Palatine."

Her polite, reserved manner returned. She withdrew the hand offering me the portrait and placed it on a nearby table. Then, she went to a window and stood looking out, her back to me. "Tell me what you want to," she said, without turning around.

"First of all, as I said, you can still change your mind. Nothing is set until the agreements have been completed and signed, and even afterward, until the marriage itself takes place. It does become more difficult the longer it goes on, but I am sure at this time your choice would be respected by both your father and brother. It is not too late."

She neither spoke nor turned around. But she did sigh and rest her head against the windowpane.

I continued, "Of most importance is whether the marriage can bring you joy and fulfilment, within the responsibilities of authority that God asks of those in our positions." I picked up the portrait from the table and brought it to her, opening it and holding it close to the window, so she could at least see part of it. "Look again at this face. Is it not one of a man you could love?"

"It's but a face. I know nothing of the man."

"Do you know any more of Count Palatine? You do not. I am told he is not nearly as handsome."

She leaned away from the window to face me. "Do you imagine me so lacking in mind as to make such a decision by looks alone? Even were each man present before me, I would never do so!" She waved a hand disdainfully towards the portrait. "Everyone knows how unreliable a portrait can be. You yourself told me the sad story of Anne of Cleves."

"Another German marriage that did not succeed," I said warningly. "Let that guide you."

She stared at me in disbelief. Then, she said quietly, "It would seem, Your Majesty my mother, that you wish me to follow your opinion, and not my own."

"I want for you not to meekly follow what the king wants for you."

"I can assure you, I don't. I have sought and received many reports of Count Palatine's character and disposition, his likes and dislikes, and his behaviour, with peers and subordinates as well as with family. Everything I've heard recommends him, and I believe us compatible. For what it's worth, we have exchanged portraits and found nothing to complain of. Our marriage holds excellent promise of being a good one. Of course, I don't delude myself that I love him, or him, me. But I do believe that in time that could happen for us, as I've been told it may, with marriages of this type. I can hope."

What she said impressed me in ways I had not expected, and I was momentarily distracted. "I do love your father," I said, almost in a contradictory way. "Although at times it has not been easy to."

"I never said you didn't," she said with distinct sympathy.

There was an awkward silence, during which we both turned and looked out the window. Then, I said, "When we came to England from Scotland, it was like entering a world of beauty and comfort after a world of severity. Your father said it was like leaving a hard bench for a soft bed. That, I imagine, is how the Palatinate of the Rhine compares to the Duchy of Savoy. Do not days of long sunlight and soft climate and gardens so close to the Mediterranean hold any allure for you? A land of the cultured ancient Latins, as opposed to the barbaric tribes of Germany? You talk of love and your hope for it. Would it not have a greater chance to prosper in such a place? Would you not be more comfortable there?"

She took a step away from the window and me, and then another, and would have retreated further had I not grabbed her wrist, saying, "Victor Amadeus would make you a fine husband, and your chances of love would be no less with him. Here, take his portrait, and at least please me by viewing it a few times before I leave." I tried again to give it to her, but she refused to take it. "All things are equal between him and Count Palatine," I insisted.

She broke free from my grasp. "You know they are not," she answered with resentment. "He is Catholic. And I must navigate the storms of religion in my life as you have in yours." She turned and started to leave the room. At the door, she stopped and looked back at me, and I saw she was on the verge of tears. "I am mystified as to why you have asked me this at all. I can only think some other reason you haven't told me has prompted you to it." She curtsied, as though I were only the queen and not her mother, and opened the door and went out, leaving me holding the portrait she would not take.

Anna came in, her face showing unease. "As she passed me, the princess asked angrily if this was my handiwork. She wouldn't even stay to hear my reply."

"She thinks me a secret Catholic, and that it is why I am encouraging the Savoy marriage. She is mistaken."

"I have never sought to lead you," Anna said defensively.

"You have not. No one has. But they all think me a fool. The conversation did not go well at all. But when she has had time to consider it, it may go better. Do not concern yourself with what she said. She knows you love her like a daughter."

I hoped Elizabeth might return, since it felt strange to have parted unhappily, which we never had before. But she did not, and the next time I saw her was outside for the riding exercise she'd invited me to. I took it as a good sign that she hadn't cancelled it, and I fully intended to continue our discussion, hoping that now the initial surprise had worn off, she would be more agreeable. But when I arrived by the stables where Lord Harrington was waiting with a horse for me, I found her already mounted on one, speaking intently to the Countess of Bedford on another beside her, with the attendants a short distance away, also mounted. Elizabeth saw me first and must have told the countess, who looked quickly towards me. Although their faces showed nothing, the startled way the countess had turned suggested that Elizabeth had been telling her of our earlier conversation.

The horse was docile, and Lord Harrington remarked it was one of the easiest in the stable, as two grooms helped me on. I was grateful for the choice, for I didn't ride nearly as much as I used to. But riding was a skill one never forgot once learned, and as I rode the short distance towards Elizabeth and the countess, I felt pleased to be taking part in something I so enjoyed. Too much of my life in recent years had been spent indoors, instead of in parks and woodlands and meadows. Life could be so much nicer when one often had access to such places, another reason recommending the Savoy marriage, for the German winters were long and cold, and one of Elizabeth's favourite pastimes was riding. Telling her so would be a good way of reintroducing the topic, after I'd drawn her away from the countess to ride beside me alone.

But Elizabeth would not look at me as I drew near, and just as I reached her and the countess, she rode off quickly, across a lawn towards the park. All around there were exclamations of surprise, and the countess said in a low voice, "She is troubled, Your Majesty, after your talk this morning."

I knew I had to go after her. Immediately, I shook the reins and followed as fast as she had ridden. I could see her growing ever smaller in the distance. "Your Majesty!" I heard voices calling out behind me, and I sensed others had followed. It was inadvisable, I knew, for me to ride so fast on a new horse over unfamiliar terrain, and my women, knowing I was out of practice, must have been greatly concerned. And yet, I continued my pursuit.

There was an opening in the trees where the park began at the end of the lawn, the start of a wide path, and Elizabeth rode into it and out of view. I followed quickly, but the path turned in an unexpected way, and the next thing I knew I'd been thrown from the saddle and was on the ground, tumbling to one side. Startled but without pain, I came to a stop in a stretch of soft grass. My hat was gone and my riding outfit a dishevelled mess, but I was unhurt. Strangely, finding myself so was appealing, and instead of standing I pressed my face against the grass and felt and smelled the spring earth beneath. It was comforting, and I felt I could stay there for hours, but I knew I could not, for already there were cries and troubled voices as the others behind me arrived and saw what had happened. In an instant, I was surrounded by my women, and then Lord Harrington and the countess, both kneeling beside me and telling me to lie still. "I'm fine," I tried to explain, but they would not be reassured, and told me to wait until a litter arrived to transport me back to the house.

Then Elizabeth appeared, someone having ridden ahead and called her back. "Mother!" she cried in alarm at the sight of me on the ground. She pushed between the countess and Lord Harrington to kneel as close to me as possible.

"I'm fine," I repeated. "It was only a silly mishap. The ground is soft."

"I didn't know you were following!" She covered her face with her hands and began to sob. "I'll never forgive myself for riding off so fast like that!"

"I was the foolish one," I insisted. Around me, I heard many of my women crying. "You must tell them I have not suffered any injury at all. Go, Elizabeth, and speak to them."

Standing, she composed herself and went to them. At the same time, the household physician appeared, leading a number of stewards and grooms through the crowd of women and horses on the path. He asked for permission to examine me, and then expertly and swiftly went about it, asking brief questions as he did. "God protects you, Your Majesty," he then said with relief. "This could have been so much worse for you."

The grooms came forward with a small litter, which they gently lifted me onto. As they did, I caught sight of my horse standing to one side, the reins held by a groom. I looked at Lord Harrington and said, "The fault was not the horse's but mine. It would displease me should there be consequences for it."

"There will be none," he replied, understanding it had been a command.

The women had stopped crying, although their faces showed deep distress as they stood back to let the litter pass. Everyone was now mostly quiet, except for the occasional hushed voice of Lord Harrington as he gave orders to the men carrying the litter. Next to me, on either side, were Elizabeth and the countess, but neither spoke. In the silence, I became aware of the birdsong in the surrounding trees. As I listened to it, I suddenly knew I should press Elizabeth no further to make a change in her choice of husband. Her riding away from me had been a clear indication that she did not want to.

Back at the house, I was carried to my room, where I was finally allowed to stand and walk about, to the physician's satisfaction. But he then instructed that I was to immediately retire and remain in bed for the next day.

When we were alone, Anna, who had met the litter halfway across the lawn, said, "You rode faster than you should have. Earlier today you said others think you a fool. They do not. But do not start giving them reason to."

"I could not stand my daughter fleeing from me! I hadn't understood how I had disturbed her earlier. It's no excuse, I know. I did so without thinking. But now, the issue is closed, unless she speaks of it again."

Later when Elizabeth came in to see me, she began to apologise, but I stopped her. For a tense moment she waited silently, as though prepared for me to resume trying to convince her of the merits of Victor Amadeus. When I instead asked about her riding, simple questions about how far she went into the countryside and how often, she became more relaxed. Half an hour later, when she left, it was clear she was grateful that my thoughts had changed direction, and I was relieved the harmony between us had been restored. But even so, I felt some disappointment and resentment that my opinion had not been heeded.

The remainder of the visit passed pleasantly and without incident, with any mention of Victor Amadeus carefully avoided by both Elizabeth and myself. Once, when I asked about a locket she was wearing, she replied that it contained a miniature of Frederick, Count Palatine. She hesitantly began to offer to show it to me, but when I changed the subject, she put it away.

By the time I left, I had decided that in future it would be better to remain an admired and respected semi-recluse at Denmark House, than to be treated as irrelevant by those who were still important. The ease with which James had dismissed me during my last visit was still fresh in my thoughts. Having failed with Elizabeth also, I had to tell Henry I could not help him, which of course would demonstrate to him how ineffectual a queen I was.

In the coach, after an hour's travel, I finally spoke to the countess of my attempt to change who Elizabeth would marry. "I believe my daughter may have told you of our conversation the morning I fell from my horse. You likely have questions about why I did. And you may feel hurt I did not confide in you that it was my main reason for this visit, and wonder why I did not. But you are too respectful to have asked, no matter how important it was to you."

"I have wanted to," she replied, deferentially. "But you know I could not. I did think, though, that in time you would tell me."

We were sitting side by side in the coach, so as to both be facing the direction we were travelling in as we rode along. But now, she switched to the seat opposite me, still not asking, although the expression on her face was questioning. I leaned back. "Henry visited me at Denmark House," I began, and proceeded to tell her of his request, and of my unsatisfactory conversation with James at Whitehall. "And so," I concluded, "I thought I could still be of some assistance to my children — Elizabeth as much as Henry, for had I liked the German marriage I would not have tried to dissuade her from it. But I did not like it, and now I dislike it even more. I am convinced she would be better off in Savoy then the Palatinate."

"She told me she desires the marriage with Frederick. It's not only for the political ambitions of the king. She wants it herself."

"Then so be it. I am done with it. Let her become Goodwife Palatine."

"I find it admirable that you sought to help young Henry. I can sympathise with his not wanting to marry a Catholic. Can you not approach the king again to argue against it? Many times, you've told me he takes more easily to the opinions of others before his mind is decided. He might very well be more attentive if he sees that you think it important enough to try again."

There was sincerity in her advice, and genuine concern for the welfare of my entire family. But her marriage was very different from mine; her husband valued her opinions and often sought them. They also had no children, and she had no experience of the tensions that could exist between parents because of them.

I looked away from her, out the window at the passing spring landscape. I pictured James's face and remembered how he had made me feel during our last meeting. "No," I replied. "I cannot ask him again."

16

The Secretary, as expected, left the world at the end of May, and was buried with great honour in recognition of his many years of service to the country. With his departure went any slight hope I'd still held that he might recover and provide Henry — and the rest of us — with assistance. Almost immediately, despite having been expected, his absence caused me anxiety, as though I'd been cast adrift. Anything I did, or thought to do, felt inadequate.

Soon after my return from Coombe Abbey, I had written Henry a note saying I had attempted what he'd asked of me, but without success. His reply had been a thank-you, but nothing more. I could now only hope that the bride James would choose for him would be Reformed.

I attempted to reassure myself that, even if a Catholic was chosen, it might be for the best. Henry, after all, would not be leaving the country like Elizabeth, so there would be very little change in his routines and daily life. His obstinate dislike of the Catholics might even be softened by such a marriage, and ultimately make him a better king. It was still a little mystifying to me that with James and I both being moderate about the religious divide except when politics demanded otherwise, Henry's beliefs were so one-sided.

Meanwhile, plans for Elizabeth's marriage to Count Palatine continued, with news of the terms of the agreement reaching me slowly at Denmark House. Nine Englishmen and six Germans were involved in negotiating it; the English dowry was to be forty thousand pounds, to be paid in full within two years of the marriage. One thousand five hundred a year would be provided by the count for her expenses, and ten thousand more if she survived him. The count would bear the expense of fifty English men and women for her household, and James would pay for the initial journey as far as the Rhine. Even I had to admit the Germans were being generous, and seemed intent on giving Elizabeth a comfortable life. But the term that stood out the most for me was that the King of England would have to agree to the marriages of any children that came of the union. Although Elizabeth had said she was making her own choice, and the countess had assured me of it, I remained doubtful that politics hadn't played the largest part. James, used to having his own way for important decisions, was seeking to control future ones.

For a time, things were quiet in Henry's household at St. James's Palace. But anything unusual there quickly became known in the city, and one morning in June I learned he had received a magnificent gift of fifteen small bronze statues from the Grand Duke of Tuscany. "The Grand Duke is shrewd," I told the Countess of Bedford when she visited later in the day. "He's heard of Henry's reputation as a collector. The gift shows the sophistication of Tuscany as well as the Medici wealth. It's clear he's trying to get his attention."

She told me that talk about it at Whitehall had already begun. "The duke's sister, Caterina de Medici, is unmarried and the same age as the prince. It's expected the Tuscan ambassador should shortly express interest in a marriage. The Medici family have more money than anyone in Europe. The dowry would be impressive."

"They are Catholic. And they have strong ties to their neighbour, the Pope, which Henry would detest even more."

"The king may find the match suitable. You know how he doesn't want any alliance that could draw England into a foreign war. My husband says the duke is very different from the Duke of Savoy, who has schemes and ambitions. This one wants only the prestige of a Medici as future Queen of England. They seek to overcome their merchant origins by becoming part of a ruling dynasty. Their attempt in France came to nothing."

In the last century, Catherine de Medici had married the French king and produced three sons who had each ruled but left no heirs, and the throne had passed to a different branch of the royal family. Each of those three kings had struggled with the religious divisions of the times, which had been, it was generally thought, worsened by their mother's interference. I said, "Many in this country would not welcome even the possibility of a repetition here of the poor decisions of a Medici queen."

"Yes, by all reports Catherine de Medici was difficult with everyone."

"Even Mary Stuart met her match in her." James's mother had been Queen of France when married to one of the sons, who had died after a reign of barely more than a year. Very deftly, her mother-in-law had then quickly arranged her return to Scotland.

"This Caternia might be quite different," the countess said. "She's from Florence, reportedly one of the most beautiful cities ever, a centre of learning and all the arts. She's lived all her life surrounded by it, and it has to have had an effect. Surely, she is both educated and refined. She might be exactly the type of bride best suited to the prince — very different from some land-seeking duke's daughter. There may be qualities that would help him come to terms with her being Catholic."

"Perhaps so," I said after a moment. "You said the Tuscan ambassador is expected to seek an audience with James? Let me know as soon as he does, along with anything you can find out about James's response."

"Would you speak favourably of it to the prince?" she asked delicately. She'd heard me say I wouldn't interfere again.

"Although I am reluctant to, I might."

But by the time I heard back from her that the marriage was being seriously considered, I had decided I would. The Medici family were avid collectors of art, curiosities and objects of scientific interest; their palaces were filled with them in much the way Henry had been filling his. Mutual interests might be just the thing to shift Henry's attitude towards a Catholic wife, especially where such a match would enhance his status as a champion of culture. And the dowry would be enormous, providing enough Medici gold to expand his own prized collections. All things considered, it was worthwhile for me to once more see if I could help bring the marriage about. At the end of June, I sent him a message asking to see the new statues, and a time was arranged for the next day.

I chose to ride the entire way to St. James's Palace, rather than travel by coach, either fully or partly after going by barge to Whitehall first. The fact that my riding skills had deteriorated so much that I had suffered the fall at Coombe Abbey had troubled me, and since returning I had ridden out a few times to improve them. Today, a small retinue accompanied me, including enough guards to ensure the inevitable crowds rushing out to see me remained at a respectful distance. I was, though, pleased by their enthusiastic cheering as I passed. As we entered St. James's Park, the foliage in full summer bloom along the drive to the palace held a promise of good things for the future.

The crenellated octagonal towers of the palace's gatehouse became visible in the distance, and a few minutes later we arrived at the redbrick Tudor building. In the courtyard I looked for the decorative H&A, for Henry VIII and Anne Boleyn, which that king had included when he'd had the palace built. Ruefully, I thought it now a reminder of the fickleness and uncertainty of life, for no matter how permanently and lovingly those initials had been set into the building, King Henry had rid himself of his second wife not long after its completion.

Henry met me, stepping past the grooms to help me dismount. He said, "Such an honour for you to visit. My apologies Charles is not here also. He has not yet completed the tasks his tutors have set for him today, so I had him remain at them. I was sure you would approve. He's to join us later."

"Your exertions for his education are laudable. The king and I are both grateful. But you must remember to be patient with him, Henry. He doesn't have your abilities."

"He makes efforts. What more can God expect of any of us?" His reply was strange, not what I would have expected. It was as though he was exceedingly aware of himself.

I'd intended to go directly to his art gallery where the duke's statues would be, but instead, I decided to try to lighten the mood with something less serious. "Now that I'm here, I find I would like to see your menagerie first."

The quickness of how he looked at me told me he was surprised, although his expression revealed nothing. "Certainly," he replied, and offered his arm to escort me to it.

On the way, he told me he kept only birds, which he enjoyed most of all. He had no desire to compete with the Tower Zoo and its many large animals. "So we have no bear-baiting or lion fights here. Although my father enjoys them, I never have. I mean no criticism of his exemplary character when I say it has always struck me as an inconsistency in him. For a man of peace who detests the battlefield, it is a brutal pastime."

"He finds it similar to the sport of the hunt, which he so enjoys. I do also."

"The older I get," Henry said pensively, "the more meaningless I find the hunt."

"There is skill and strategy involved."

A number of his courtiers were close enough to hear us, a small audience he was aware of. I was sure his comments were for them as much as me, as he continued, "Riding after a helpless, inferior beast now strikes me as unfair. Beasts being pitted against each other for our amusement seems equally unworthy and cruel. The only object of man's aggression should be other men, where matters of principle and righteousness are involved. Had my father taken up his predecessor's opposition to the Spanish instead of making peace with them, and led England to more glorious victories like that over the armada, his interest in the hunt and bear-baiting might have been redirected into the creation of the better world he so desires." Even more assertively, he added, "Which it can never be, with Spain so dominant."

"As you said, the king is a man of peace. He does as he believes he must."

"As must we all."

"He is admired for it."

Henry did not reply, and for a while neither of us spoke as we continued on, our pace neither hurried nor slow. His not having said anything disparaging about the Catholics generally was encouraging for what I wanted to achieve during the visit. He would never, I understood, moderate his hatred of the Spanish, and when he became king, it was likely he would fight them. Already, he supported the Virginia colony in the Americas as the first foothold to curtail Spanish expansion, as well as the search for a northern passage to break their control of the trade routes. But so long as he could distinguish between Spain and other Catholics, things might not turn out badly. Those of the Italian states, despite the presence of the Pope, might be tolerable to him. Henry had too much intellect not to grasp that the ambitions of those states, although Catholic, were also obstructed by Spain. Hopefully he would understand that marriage with Caternia de Medici might be of great assistance in the accomplishment of his future plans.

In the menagerie, his manner softened as we walked past the cages, his speech slower and appreciative. He spoke of the occupants of each, the tall ostriches, black and white American chickens, colourful pheasants, a large eagle, turtle doves, and an entirely white parrot. Most remained indifferent as we passed, except for the parrot, who appeared pleased to see Henry as he opened a little door on the cage and extended his hand in. The parrot flew to it, and Henry brought him out, perched on his wrist. Although my women drew even further back behind me, I stayed beside him. Parrots, I'd heard, could be tamed, and I doubted it was dangerous. And Henry hadn't warned us to be careful, as he had when we'd passed the ostriches, which, despite their elegant beauty, could reach through the bars and bite those who came too close.

The way he held the parrot close and lovingly touched its white feathers was charming. "Can it talk?" I asked. "I've heard they can be taught to."

"He doesn't. I've tried to teach him, as have some of the handlers, but without success. I don't find it much of a disappointment. When they do, it's not thoughtful speech, only repetitions of sounds they have learned. I do not find us humans so admirable as to be imitated. Better for us to appreciate the unintelligible noises they make." He put the parrot back in its cage, where it flew from his hand to its feeding dish. After he'd closed and secured the little door, he turned to me and asked, "Would you have me be a parrot, and simply repeat the ideas of others? A prince, and then a king, with no mind of his own?"

Behind me, my women and his courtiers were abruptly silent. He'd spoken loudly enough for them to hear, apparently wanting them to.

"Certainly not," I answered. "Always you must think for yourself. Yet there can be wisdom in what others have to tell us."

He stared at me searchingly before saying, "Come, you are here to see my gifts from the Grand Duke of Tuscany. Let us go."

As we left, a shriek rang out in the menagerie, bringing fearful exclamations from my women. I looked with concern at Henry.

"The parrot," he said mildly. "Although he doesn't talk, he reminds us of his presence."

The art was in the palace's three-sided long gallery, around one of the courtyards. Since my last visit the collection had grown considerably and was unlike any I'd seen in Scotland or England, with magnificent large paintings of sea and land battles, and mythological and religious scenes, as well as others of common folk in ordinary settings. Again, as he had with his birds, Henry spoke in detail about each work, also telling me of its artist, and where in Europe it had come from. It was clear he took great pride in having them, with a deep appreciation of not only their beauty but their value. The dreamlike mood that came over him was fascinating to me, of much more interest than the art we were passing. But then, something began to seem awkward about it. We were nearly at the end of the gallery when, with sudden clarity, I saw the similarity to how I responded to my jewellery collection. And I knew for the first time that it had been meant to replace the love absent from my life.

I looked away from Henry and the pictures, to the floor. He was only eighteen, at the start of his life. That he should already feel such emptiness was nearly unbearable for me to acknowledge.

"Here are the duke's statues," Henry said, as we left the pictures and approached where they were displayed on a long table. Even with the distraction of my inner turmoil I was able to appreciate the beauty of the fifteen bronzes, gorgeously shaped as figures from the ancient world. Most were from myths, and some were of animals. Leaving my side, Henry went closer, and after briefly contemplating them, shifted the positions of some. "Although each one stands as a work of merit on its own, they are most impressive as a group," he told me thoughtfully, still studying the effect of the rearrangement.

It was time to come to the purpose of my visit. "Henry," I said, "I must speak with you alone. Can we leave the others here for a while?" Encouraging him towards the Tuscan marriage was now of even greater importance. His best chance of overcoming the emptiness he was filling with pets and art was in finding love with a wife who was his peer in intellect and sensitivity, which might ensure its continuation over the years. Beyond hunting, James and I had never shared interests, his intellectual pursuits boring me and my artistic ones, him. If we had, we might not now be so estranged from each other.

Henry showed no surprise at the request. He said, "Let's go to the library, then. The others can continue to enjoy the gallery or the gardens." On the way, he told me that while there were many visitors to his gallery, the library was seen by few. "The only one who uses it besides myself and Charles and his tutors is our chaplain. He does so to great effect, and his daily sermons are erudite. The difference from those at Whitehall is notable. I know, because often after hearing ours, I cross the park and attend the one there. Although disappointing, I feel I benefit from the second one."

"Who would not?" I replied politely, and at once began to speak of the benefits of crossing the park twice instead. Some might find the depth of Henry's religious commitment in attending two morning sermons admirable, but for me it was an obstacle to a Catholic marriage, and I wanted to avoid discussing it further. Neither did I want to veer into talking of my own chaplain's sermons at Denmark House, for these days I often did not attend.

The library was as impressive as the art gallery, a long, panelled room with cupboards and shelves holding, Henry told me proudly, nearly two thousand books. But when he began describing the contents of each section as we started down the aisle on one side of the shelves dividing the room, his manner was methodical and clear, unlike how he'd been with his art. He was apprehensive of what I had to say, and not allowing himself to be distracted from his readiness for it.

I drew a deep breath, knowing already the conversation could be difficult. "The statues are lovely," I began, "surpassing my expectations. Florence must be a wonderous place, to produce such fine artists. I have been told the Grand Duke patronises many of them, and also men of science. The gold of the Medici family has been well spent improving the world."

"It has," he agreed.

I stopped walking and turned to face him. "I have also been told the Grand Duke has a sister. And that he has approached your father with a request for a marriage between you."

"Yes," he said mildly. "He has." There was not the slightest change in his manner. He looked away from me, leaning towards a shelf as though to better see the several books on it.

There was no longer any reason to avoid being direct. "I am sure you have already surmised the reason I am here."

"You want me to marry Caterina de Medici." He continued to look at the books.

"I want you to consider it. At least look at her portrait."

"I have. It was sent to the Tuscan ambassador here at the same time the statues were to me. The Grand Duke is concisely efficient."

"And how did you find her?"

"She is beautiful," he answered, without commitment. Finally, he turned his face towards me, his alert blue eyes staring into mine. "But her beauty wouldn't be at issue, would it? Even if she had none." Before I could answer, he moved further down the aisle, saying, "Let us be frank with each other, Mother."

I followed him. "I am trying to be."

Opposite the shelves were mostly cupboards. He stopped before one and opened its centre panel forward and downward, showing a number of smaller doors and drawers inside.

"These are my wonder cabinets," he said, traces of his earlier entranced mood seeming about to emerge again. "This one contains some of my most valued treasures. They come from the farthest corners of the earth." He started to open one of the smaller drawers as if to show me its contents, but then abruptly closed it. An instant later, the outer panel was back in place also.

Holding off a sense of rejection at having been pushed away, I said, "The Medici family are great collectors."

"And they wish to add a prince to their collection," he said, with the scorn and disdain he must have felt all along.

"You did not return the duke's gift. Surely you knew what would follow."

"And surely you know that politics would not allow me to return it. Besides that, the statues are beautiful, and I want them. I can accept them as a sign of the duke's friendship, and that of Tuscany. But I cannot take a Catholic as a wife. No matter how beautiful or culturally accomplished — which I assume would be what you wish to convince me of today — or how much Medici wealth or political benefit would follow, I cannot."

Unable to stop myself, I exclaimed, "How can you be so small-minded? This attitude is not fitting for a future king! There is so little difference between Catholic and Reformed belief!"

"There is a vast difference," he said with steady calmness. "As I am sure the Pope and the papists would agree."

"Common ground exists. You have only to seek it! You could become an example of a peace which could follow for all of Europe."

"No. It is not who I am. All of Europe already sees in me a leader for the Reformed. I believe it is what God wants of me. For years I have been certain of it. It is part of my soul, as a man, a prince, and a future king. To take a Catholic as a wife would go against the very centre of my being. It would be intolerable for me."

He had spoken carefully, but there was something terrible about the chiselled calculation of his tone. I decided to try to appeal to something gentler. "Caterina de Medici is from one of the most refined places on earth, where the best of human endeavour is appreciated. She could not possibly herself be otherwise, like some dull or foolish princess from a backward European state. Everything about her holds promise of being a woman you could love. Do you not think that having such a wife would enable you to better understand what God wants of you, and to do his work? The religious difference could be a minor matter that recedes into the background. Surely an initial agreement could be reached for her to practise her faith only privately in her rooms. There would be no diminishment of the role you seek for yourself in the Reformed world."

"It would be a statement to the world of the emptiness of my beliefs," he replied. "No, I could not abide it."

"You may have no choice, if the king decides otherwise."

"There are always choices," he said meaningfully.

"Choices? What choices?"

He hesitated, then said, "I have been assured I would be welcomed in Germany as a unifying leader against the Hapsburgs, should I choose to go there."

"Henry! You would never seriously consider such a thing?"

He stared at me, then went to the end of the aisle and around to the other side, leaving me alone. A moment later I joined him, where he was once more studying the books on a shelf. "These are all about the Orient," he said, as though it had been the subject of our conversation.

Ignoring the remark, I said, "You must never leave the country until you are king, and even after that only if there is an unavoidable necessity to do so. The English people — and the Scottish — love you and look to you for their future prosperity. Your becoming entangled in affairs abroad might alienate them."

He began walking down the aisle, looking at the shelves, and I stayed right behind him. Then, he turned around. "I do not want to go," he said. "I hope I am not placed in a position where I would feel I had to."

"Even if at first you do not like the bride chosen, you should not go. You are young, and feelings are subject to change over time."

We were back where we had started, having fully circled the centre shelves. I wanted to reassure myself that the possibility of his going to Germany had been no more than an unpleasant passing thought, but right then Charles came in, with his tutor and two attendant gentlemen. Although my thoughts were still fixed on what his brother had said, I was taken by how strong and confident he looked as he bowed smoothly to me, without tottering or losing his balance as he once might have. The Careys' efforts had been continued in Henry's household, and Charles was now barely recognisable as the same child who had arrived from Scotland.

"We looked for you in the gallery but were told you were here," he said in a clear voice, sounding older than his eleven years.

Henry, after being told the lessons had been satisfactorily completed, dismissed the tutor and attendants. I gestured for Charles to come closer and bent forward for him to kiss my cheek, which he did, respectfully but a little shyly.

"Your brother tells me you make good use of this library," I said, trying to sound friendly. But it was difficult to think of anything other than Henry's suggestion of leaving the country.

"I do," Charles answered, while Henry half smiled approvingly. He so seldom smiled that it was satisfying to see. I saw the promise of his ability as a father when he had children of his own.

"It's one of his favourite rooms here," Henry said. "But I believe he likes the menagerie also." To Charles, he said, "Her Majesty our mother requested to see it, and we visited it before the gallery."

"And how did you like the new statues from Italy?" Charles asked.

"They are wonderful additions to your brother's collections."

"They are," Henry agreed appreciatively. "Shall we go see them again, Mother? You barely did before."

"Not today," I replied. "I saw what I came to — and some other things I had not expected."

17

In September, I finally breathed a sigh of relief upon learning that the proposed marriage between Henry and Caterina de Medici had failed. The unresolvable issue had been the Pope's insistence upon any children of the union being raised as Catholics, which James had found unacceptable. Henry, who during the months of negotiations had maintained a calm, reserved attitude, responded to the news with a noticeable display of good cheer, which increased even more when we heard Count Palatine would arrive in England by mid-October. But his mood again darkened, and my anxiety returned, when James and his counsellors began reconsidering the previously rejected marriage for him with the daughter of the Catholic Duke of Savoy.

I again began to dread he might leave for Germany if pressed to accept the match. This time it seemed even more likely that he would, for the proposed bride had none of the cultural attractions of the previous one with her illustrious Medici background. But when I tried to think of new reasons to offer to as a deterrent to his leaving, I found none. My knowledge of the subtleties of European politics was insufficient to present anything remotely convincing to someone with his intellect, and I had already seen the futility of an emotional appeal in my earlier attempt. Repeating to James what he had told me about the invitation from the Germans to lead their opposition to the Catholic Hapsburgs could have disastrous personal results, destroying their familial bond. I couldn't imagine what might follow, should James feel threatened politically. I despaired of the absence of the Secretary, for there was no one else I could speak to without the possibility of James learning of it, which would be more problematic than if I told him myself.

With the approach of Count Palatine, Elizabeth's marriage was set for November, before the start of Advent. Plans began for magnificent festivities at Whitehall, starting with a pageant of a sea battle involving forty vessels on the Thames, on the eve of the wedding. The next day would be the ceremony in the chapel, with Elizabeth attended by twenty noblemen's daughters, and then a banquet in the Great Hall, with dancing and music. More feasting would follow the next day, and a tournament in the tiltyard by the noblemen of England and those of the count's retinue, and a masque.

Given that my interest in masques was known to everyone, I expected to be asked to oversee it, although I was not sure I wanted to be more than minimally involved with the festivities in any way, since I disliked the marriage. But I was surprised when James arrived at Denmark House to make the request personally.

"I know you've considered this marriage beneath our daughter," he said, but not unpleasantly, as soon as we were alone in the sitting room where I greeted him. "You had hoped for the King of Spain to become her husband."

I looked at him in a way that didn't deny it, but signalled I was resigned to it. I was flattered he had appeared himself to ask me to participate.

He continued, "Count Palatine is one of the most important men in Europe." He smiled indulgently as his eyelids half-closed. "She is to be far more than Goodwife Palatine." So, he had heard of my use of the expression to explain my disdain for the marriage. It seemed to amuse him.

I said, "I know it is what she wants. I pray to God for the marriage's success."

"We all do. And so we should provide them with as perfect a wedding as possible at the outset. For that, Anne, your involvement is needed. There is to be a masque. Who is better suited to see that it is perfect? No one, certainly not me. You are talented in ways I am not, and this is one of them."

I had thought he found the masques not only tedious but slightly ridiculous, and I now appreciated the compliment from him. "Of course, I agree," I said. He was making more of an effort to be agreeable and respectful than he had in months, and I would respond accordingly. "Have whoever in your household is supervising the festivities contact me. Sooner rather than later, and we had best begin at once."

"Dear Anne," he said, "I knew I could rely on you."

I asked if he would stay for dinner, but he said no, he was required back at Whitehall. I would have liked him to stay, but was still satisfied that the visit had been made solely for conferring with me. We spoke of unimportant things as I accompanied him outside across the terrace to where his barge waited. Briefly, I considered telling him of what Henry had said about leaving for Germany if a Catholic bride was chosen for him, which was still in my thoughts nearly every day. But I decided not to. If things continued so nicely between us, I might find the right time for it later.

Detailed plans for the masque were sent to me the next day. The theme was to be the marriage of Thames and Rhine, celebrated on Mount Olympus, using characters from Greek mythology in tableaux and dances. Different parts of the mountain would be shown, with statues of gold and silver coming to life. It was to be more elaborate than any I'd been involved with, and I immediately realised I would have to go to Whitehall myself if I was to make any meaningful contribution.

*

Several days later I was met there in the Great Hall by the Countess of Bedford, and numerous costume and scenery designers, most of whom I knew from other masques I'd participated in. The entire afternoon was then spent in my providing advice for the staging of what was to be a very complicated presentation. The genuine interest in my opinions and suggestions from everyone was gratifying, and I knew I had made the right decision to agree to assist them.

In the midst of one discussion, Henry came in unannounced with attendant gentlemen, causing everyone to step back and bow. "I did not know you were to be at Whitehall today," I said, pleasantly surprised, as he and his gentlemen reached me and bowed.

"Neither did I know you would be," he answered. "Although I must say the business of state that brought me was of less interest than what has brought you. I see faces I recognise here. The talent promises an excellent result."

Unlike James, he had an interest in masques and had staged admirable ones, so of course he would have known many of the people working on the new one. "Your recommendations would be welcome, if you care to stay a while," I said.

I could only wonder if the state business he had been called for was to do with negotiations for his marriage. There had been no definite news regarding the Duke of Savoy's daughter, other than that those negotiations were continuing. But I'd heard other talk of a possible marriage with a Scottish noblewoman, proposed by those who wanted deeper ties between England and Scotland. Should I have the chance to speak favourably of a Scottish bride, I might do so, but today was not the time for it.

"I can't stay," Henry replied regretfully. Looking around the hall, he then suggested stands be created along the walls for the crowd who would want to see the masque. "As many as possible should be accommodated. This marriage is popular among both the nobility and commoners, as I knew it would be. Almost everyone approves of it, except the Catholics."

He then coughed deeply, and I saw how pale he was, as though he might have been unwell for a few days. I knew that if it had been serious, I would have heard about it already, but it still concerned me. I waited the few minutes until he left, then quietly asked the countess to follow and see what she could learn from his gentlemen.

I was inspecting samples of cloth for the costumes in the masque's pastoral part when she returned, waving the others off while she spoke to me. She said, "He's had a cold for several days, which it's believed he caught by swimming in the Thames. But he's improving and it should shortly be over."

"He shouldn't swim in the river at all," I answered, thankful it was only that. "And especially not in September." I turned my attention back to the cloth before me. The day was nearly over, and there was still so much to do. It was likely I'd need to return to Whitehall several times.

Later that week I received another request, this time from Elizabeth, who wanted me to take charge of the completion of her wedding dress and trousseau after she returned to Coombe Abbey, where she would stay until her future husband arrived. I agreed at once, taking it as another sign of respect and appreciation of my abilities. Denmark House then became the centre for the tailors and embroiderers creating the wardrobe of velvets, satins, tissue and lace Elizabeth would take to Germany. For the wedding, she would wear embroidered cloth of gold and silver. Over the following weeks several rooms gradually became full of the new garments, waiting for her return.

Before she had left, she had decided she would wear diamonds with her wedding dress. James and I and her brothers agreed we would make them our wedding gifts, and each of us then found our way to Mr. Heriot's shop. Although I had been eager to go, my visit failed to provide the same interest and pleasure for me that it usually did. Looking over the lovely diamond arrangements, for the first time I thought of their cost, and if things so rarely worn were worth it. But Elizabeth's attire would be reported far and wide as a representation of the Stuart dynasty, and it had to be magnificent. With that in mind, I made my choice, but in an almost indifferent way. I then found it tedious when Mr. Heriot described what James and our sons had selected. For the first time, I left his shop without buying anything for myself.

In the middle of October the small fleet belonging to Count Palatine was sighted off Gravesend, and the next day anchored there. A carefully rehearsed delegation went to welcome him, and Elizabeth was sent for. The morning before she arrived, I went by myself into the rooms where mannequins displayed the now finished dresses. They were fit for any queen, regal and expensive-looking, enough to contradict my image of Elizabeth as merely Goodwife Palatine. I had finally accepted that the position she was taking was appropriate for her, and she and her husband would play important roles in European politics. But as I walked among the mannequins, their emptiness beneath the fine garments began to disturb me. I wondered if my daughter would be able to find herself beneath the role that life was clothing her in.

The next day, the count arrived in London, greeted by a huge ovation from the crowds who flocked to the river as his barge reached the city, and a blare of trumpets at the Water Gate of Whitehall. There he was met by Charles, who brought him to where we waited in the Great Hall, surrounded by guards wearing new uniforms of golden velvet, and courtiers in their finest clothing. A great stillness took hold of me as he approached; I would not rest easily until I knew he was indeed in person everything he had been reputed to be. But, with each step that drew him closer, I saw the original matched the portraits, and other descriptions of him. He was handsome, with balanced features, although slightly darker in colouring and a bit shorter than expected. He walked with perfect poise, smoothly and easily through the crowded hall as though he had done so many times before. Reaching us, he bowed low, removing his wide-brimmed hat, and then greeted James, all the while refraining from looking at Elizabeth, standing beside me. In careful English he then offered the typical political salutation, but then, less formally, an apology for not being more grandly dressed. Only then did it occur to me that, unlike ours, his clothing was that of a traveller. He explained that the ship carrying his wardrobe had suffered a mishap and he had arrived with only what he wore. "But I could not," he said, with a touch of mirth, "delay presenting myself to my bride and her family out of fear I would be found too humbly attired."

It was exactly the right thing to say, especially to me, with the emptiness of Elizabeth's dress mannequins still in my thoughts. James, equally pleased, replied that he should say no more of it, that his eagerness to appear before us was commendable. The count then turned to me, and I saw the frank and direct look in his brown eyes. There was stability in them, and intellect, different from James's mercurial type or the seriousness of Henry's. He would be capable of forming and maintaining a marital bond with Elizabeth, and no matter what life brought to them, they would have that to sustain them. I smiled as genuinely as I could as he took my hand in his and kissed it.

He then respectfully backed away a few steps, and went to Henry, on the other side of James. Henry stepped towards him, enough for me to see their greeting, formal again, but with cordiality and familiarity, as though each recognised the kindred spirit they had hoped to find. Briefly, I was troubled by the contrast in their appearances, for Henry looked paler and less defined despite being more elaborately dressed, his fair hair insubstantial compared with the dark curls of the slightly younger count. I had heard he had still not yet fully recovered his typical good health after his illness more than a month ago, but the few times I had seen him it had not been as noticeable as it was today. After the conclusion of the day's ceremonies, I would speak to James about insisting that he have adequate rest until he was himself again.

During the greetings, Elizabeth had remained motionless beside me, and although I could not see her face, I was certain that in the same way the count had not even looked at her, her eyes had remained turned towards the floor. But as he now left Henry and came back around to her, I caught the moment when they first fully saw each other, and their satisfaction with what they were encountering. The count bowed all the way to the floor and in a show of devotion kissed the hem of Elizabeth's gown, after which she immediately curtsied. Then, they each gave a small exclamation and kissed each other. Cheers and applause resounded through the Great Hall, and hand in hand the young couple turned in every direction to acknowledge it. Despite my misgivings, the marriage was beginning well and there was every indication it would be a success. Now, I could only hope that Henry's would go the same way.

After the celebrations ended, before I departed for Denmark House, I drew James away from his attendants to speak to him alone.

"Henry looks tired to me," I said. "Could you please see that he rests sufficiently over the next week?"

"A difficult task, always. Henry has a mind of his own."

"I know. But please try."

Two days later, at a banquet I held at Denmark House in honour of the count — Frederick, as he was now called by our family — Henry looked somewhat improved, and I was confident he would soon be himself again. He had been riding with Frederick, and played cards with him, but there had been no reports of anything more, and so it seemed James had done as I requested. Meanwhile, Frederick and Elizabeth had spent as much time as they could together, and appeared completely suited to each other. During the banquet, seated side by side next to James, they seemed absorbed in each other's company, to the exclusion of almost everyone else.

While James was occupied with a group of nobility he'd called to speak with him at the table, I turned to Henry, seated beside me. I had seen to it that several of his favourite dishes were served, and watched during the many courses to ensure that he eaten them, which he had, although not as much as I would have liked. And although he still coughed occasionally, it was less frequently than before. Also, there was a steady calmness about him that I was sure had to do with satisfaction that his sister's marriage with Frederick was happening.

"Frederick meets with your approval?" I asked him. "He certainly seems to have already won that of your sister." I gestured towards where they sat.

"He does. And I believe he has won yours and the king's, also."

"So it would seem," I said agreeably.

"He is popular everywhere in the city. Crowds gather where he is expected, with everyone wanting to see him. Yesterday we almost could not ride as we wished to, so many gathered in the park, and our attendants had to intervene. The people understand the great alliance this marriage represents, between us and the countries of Northern Europe in the Reformed cause. I have played my part by supporting it."

"And what of your own marriage?" I asked, although I had not intended to. "Little news ever reaches me from Whitehall about state matters, and I have heard nothing of it."

"There are those about the king who still press for the Savoy marriage," he answered, almost as though it pertained to somebody else, not him. "But there are others against it. I believe the king's interest in it has receded, especially because of the foreign difficulties it could bring. But of importance too is that the king is now seeing the reception of Frederick here, and how favourably the people view this alliance. Surely he understands that another Reformed marriage would be best, for many reasons."

"I can only hope that whoever is chosen is as pleasing to you as Frederick is to Elizabeth." But I knew that for him, unlike her, whether that happened or not would still depend on religion. I wanted to ask again if he still entertained thoughts of going to Germany if a Catholic was chosen, but I decided against it, because if so, there was nothing I could say that I had not said already. Besides, he had said the possibility of the Savoy marriage was about to vanish, and there was no denying the favour with which the German alliance was seen. There seemed every chance that in time, all the pieces might fall into place to bring about the future all of us wanted.

It was therefore with surprise and dread that I learned the next week that James, with his advisors, had decided upon the Savoy marriage.

The news was brought to me by the Countess of Bedford, who, knowing the depth of my interest, came to Denmark House early in the morning the day after the decision was made. "In the end, it was about money," she told me directly, not caring that I saw her dislike of it. "The dowry the duke offered was a fortune. But also, the king wishes to show that England, despite his daughter's German marriage, is not fully aligning itself against the Catholic countries."

"Is the decision final?" If not, I might still be able to find a way to stop it.

"Yes. Commissioners have been appointed to finish the details with Savoy."

"Surely there is something to be done!"

"Not now. The money is needed here, and there is no chance of it being matched elsewhere. Any other dowry offered, even from the Medici family, was less."

I was taken by the feeling that I was useless, unable even to have helped my husband see the indifference he was showing to our son. "It is exactly the opposite of what Henry wants. Exactly! I never believed so little respect for him would be shown by James."

"I have heard," said the countess, "that the king did go so far as to see how devoted to Catholicism the bride is, and was satisfied to learn it did not run deeply. She has agreed to participate in our services when essential and celebrate Mass only in her own quarters. There have been reports that she believes one religion is the same as another."

For someone else it was an attitude that might make a difference, but for Henry, it wouldn't. "Henry is going to find this impossible! I would not be surprised if he has already left the country."

"He hasn't, and if he does, it won't be immediately. He's in no condition to travel. His illness has returned, and he has taken to his bed. He sent a message to Whitehall asking that the decision be delayed until he could appear in person to present his reasons against it. But it was done anyway."

"Does James believe money can make up for a marriage that begins with resentment and dislike? Or that the marriages of our children can make any meaningful difference to the struggles of religion in Europe? So much is manipulated beyond simple matters of belief, it is going to take years before any peace or accord is reached. James deludes himself about his ability to affect it!"

Wisely, the countess said nothing, but I could see from her face that she did not disagree. Even so, she shifted the topic away from criticism of James to Henry. "The prince is attended by doctors sent by the king. If there is improvement, he can attend the Guildhall banquet tomorrow in honour of the Count Palatine. His absence would cause comment about the city and suggest discord that doesn't exist."

"I intend to send my own doctors immediately. Which I should have, a month ago."

"I am certain they can be of assistance," she said reassuringly. "And I am equally sure that the prince is going to be at the Guildhall tomorrow night."

18

Henry did not recover as hoped, and it was necessary for a public announcement to be made that a minor illness had prevented him from attending the banquet. My concerns deepened after the doctors I had sent reported back to me that his symptoms were still the same. "I'm going to St. James Palace," I told Anna, "to see for myself what condition my son is in."

"After the announcement, the people might become alarmed if they see you there," she answered. "The king should be asked before you go."

I almost disregarded her, but finally saw she was right and sent a message to James. Quickly, there was a reply that our entire family would visit Henry together the next day. I was requested to go to Whitehall, from where we would leave.

The next morning, I was met at the Whitehall Water Gate by Frederick and Elizabeth, who brought me to where James was waiting with a royal coach to take us across the park to St. James's Palace. A group of courtiers and a number of the nobility prominently involved in the government were there also, on horseback, to accompany us.

"Why are they all coming with us?" I asked James, letting him see I was annoyed by their presence. "Can we not visit our son even when he is ill without such a crowd? Surely a quiet family visit would serve best. Please, dismiss them."

"No. They should see the prince also."

I had been about to enter the coach but stopped where I was, in a way that indicated I would proceed no further. This was one time I would not be told what to do when I did not agree. I said, "I can go by myself, then, after you and all of them have left."

There was silence in the crowd around us, those nearest having either heard what I had said, or realised from my stopping that something was not as it should be. James, unaccustomed to having his authority challenged even in minor ways, at first could only stare at me. But I returned the stare with determination, at the same time wondering how things between us could have so deteriorated.

Between us, but off to one side, Elizabeth and Frederick both looked uneasily from myself to James, and back again. Elizabeth's anxiety for her brother had been visible as soon as she had greeted me at the Water Gate, and Frederick appeared subdued yet alert, hovering protectively beside her. Now, both looked confused, unsure of whether to intervene or not.

Abruptly, James said, "It matters not who comes with us so long as we see him. Our visit can bolster his mood in beneficial ways and should not be delayed. Let us go now, Anne. Please."

It was not his use of the word 'please' that made me turn and enter the coach, but the reason he offered, for it told me he thought Henry was sicker than I had thus far believed. A wave of fear washed over me, which repeated when I saw for the first time that Elizabeth looked like she was about to cry as she took her seat opposite me. As James sat down beside me, I grasped his sleeve and asked him, "Is it worse than I have been told?"

"Yes, but not fatal at this time. He should recover as has been expected all along. But there are rumours he is declining, and we need to dispel them by having others see him. That is why we are accompanied by so many.. We must think of the country, although it is difficult at times like this to remember we are king and queen in addition to father and mother."

Frederick leaned forward and said to me, "Have hope, Your Majesty." But by the way Elizabeth's hand clung to his, I knew that more than that was going to be necessary.

Charles met us in the palace courtyard. "My brother is awake, and eager to see all of you," he said in a very serious and dignified manner. "Allow me to take you to him without delay." We followed even before those with us on horseback had dismounted.

The large outer room in Henry's bedroom suite was already full of his courtiers and household members, but despite their number there was not the usual loud conversation, as though they had all been speaking in hushed tones. They stepped back and bowed as we passed through quickly, but still with enough time for me to see that their faces, although not mirthful, were not stricken with grief either. For the first time since entering the coach my anxiety receded a little, for surely if the worst had been anticipated they would have shown it.

A few steps from the door to the bedroom it opened, and a doctor emerged, who I recognised as one of James's. Seeing us, he bowed and then came forward as James beckoned him. "He is very weak and complains of pain in his head," he answered when asked how Henry fared. "And he cannot stand without fainting. But he has taken both food and drink, and the potions we have prepared for him. There is still hope of his mending, in time. In the future it is imperative that he does not swim in the Thames, and takes care not to exhaust himself. I am told that a week ago, he played tennis in his shirt on a day of sharp weather." But as we went past him into the bedroom, I thought the cause of Henry's illness might have more to do with the Savoian marriage than any game of tennis.

Although the outer room, where Henry conducted most of his daily business and received guests, had been opulently decorated in a manner suiting the Prince of Wales, the inner bedroom was as starkly furnished as if it had been that of a monk. No tapestries or pictures were on the dark panelled walls, and there were no cabinets or chairs, only a single long bench. The spaciousness of the room made it appear emptier, as did the stark light from the two large windows, which were without draperies. Neither did the bed have curtains or elaborate covers. In it, Henry lay on his back, his head resting on a single pillow.

Two men, obviously physicians, who were standing at the end of the bed bowed as they saw us, and then left, as did three footmen who had been waiting behind them.

Charles went directly to the bed, ahead of us. "Brother," he said, "the king and queen are here to see you, and our sister and the Count Palatine."

From where we stood, I could see Henry stirring beneath the blanket, but Charles stopped him. "No, you must stay in bed. There is no disrespect if you do." The rest of us went closer, Charles stepping back and out of the way so we could look down at Henry.

He looked a pale shade of himself, whiter than I had ever seen him, his eyes sunken with creases at their edges and in his forehead. But seeing us, something seemed to stir in him. "Wine," he said weakly, and I was aware of Charles immediately going to the door and opening it, and speaking to the footmen on the other side. In passing, I wondered when Charles had become so efficient.

"Please forgive me for staying where I am in your presence," Henry said in a low voice, "but as you can see, I am not as you usually find me."

James and I were standing on one side of the bed, Elizabeth and Frederick on the other. James said, "You have overstrained yourself of late. But the physicians feel there is every chance of a complete return to your former self."

"A few days' rest is all I require." Even speaking seemed to require effort for him.

"Whatever is necessary," I said. "I see now you should have taken to your bed a month ago."

"My responsibilities —" he began, but James stopped him.

"The queen is right," he said, then corrected himself, "Your mother is right. Even now we see the agitation you show at the thought of it."

Behind us the door could be heard opening, followed by footsteps. Then Charles appeared beside the bed with one of the doctors and a footman, holding a pitcher and a cup of wine. Elizabeth and Frederick stepped back, and the footman gently held Henry's head so he could drink from the cup the doctor offered. I was relieved to see he finished it, which reaffirmed that the best could be expected.

Henry rested back on the pillow again, then turned to Elizabeth and Frederick, who had resumed their places as the physician and footman retreated to the other side of the room.

"My apologies for my indisposition," Henry said, his voice clearer after the wine. "I want no interference with your wedding."

"It can be delayed," Elizabeth said at once.

"Yes," echoed Frederick. "Delayed."

"The thought of my marriage without you in the ceremonies is unthinkable," she continued, sounding a little strange, as though attempting to have shifting things remain as she wanted them.

"Frederick's family would not object," James said. "Under the circumstances."

"They would not," Frederick said.

"No," Henry answered. "I am easier knowing this marriage has been accomplished."

Before any of us could continue trying to dissuade him, James changed the subject. "Henry, a number of the nobility and men from the government have accompanied us today in the hope of seeing you. It would be helpful for them to be able to. They wait in the outer room. Perhaps another cup of wine could assist you in receiving them?"

He replied that it would. At once, the doctor and footman returned, and he drank again. "Send them in," he said.

"It's time for us to leave," James then told me, Elizabeth and Frederick. "A short visit, but a reassuring one. There is no reason for us to remain when the others are here, and our presence might cause delay. The prince is in good hands and our staying can only distract him. Rest is what is most required."

It was then that I knew what I had to do, whether James liked it or not. Looking down at Henry, I said, "We understand how this marriage of your sister's pleases you. The king wants you to know that the decision about the Duke of Savoy's daughter is not to be finalised until your reasons against it have been heard. You may easily end up with a German bride instead." Turning slightly towards James, but not facing him, I asked, "Is that not so, James?"

Time seemed to have stopped until he answered, "The prince's opinions are always considered." But the way he said it was far from convincing, and as I looked down at Henry to say goodbye, I did not think he believed it.

James waited until we were in the coach before showing he was displeased by what I had said. "Henry's marriage is a matter of state. You should not interfere with it. Fortunately, there was no one present for whom what you said could make a difference."

"It would make a difference to Henry! Do you not care what he does and does not want? Are you so unaware of him as not to know he does not want the Savoy marriage?

"This discussion is over," he said. To Frederick and Elizabeth, both of whom looked as though they would have preferred to be anywhere else, he said, "Thank you for your presence today. I am sure you would agree that the prince only needs time. Perhaps it won't be necessary for your wedding to be delayed after all."

We rode the rest of the way across St. James's Park in silence, each of us turned towards the widow beside us. At the last moment after we reached Whitehall, before the coach came to a stop, I said, "You sell our son's marriage to the Savoyards.. Never would I have believed it."

The coach stopped. Without a word, James opened the door, stepped out and walked away.

Frederick, with deft graciousness, immediately held out his hand and assisted me out, and then Elizabeth. As our attendants gathered around us, she asked if I would come to her rooms in the palace. "I would so appreciate your company," she said sincerely, but I knew she was thinking I might be needing hers.

"No," I said. "I want to go back to Denmark House. Where, apparently, I belong."

The next day, there were reports that Henry was somewhat better after our visit. "Be of good cheer, Your Majesty," Anna said to me after hearing them. "The prince has the best of care. No doubt that time should set things right with him."

But a dark feeling of failure and impending loss had taken hold of me after returning to Denmark House, and despite the good news I was unable to throw it off. Because of it, I decided to wait a day before going to see Henry again, which I intended to do this time on my own, without seeking James's permission. Meanwhile, I tried to bring myself out of it by attempting to view my jewellery collection, but even the first case felt meaningless, and I didn't continue. I had my women cancel the entertainment planned for that evening and went to bed, hoping I would wake in the morning feeling differently.

The next day I felt the same but resolved to go anyway. We were in the courtyard ready to depart on horseback when a message came from Whitehall saying the prince's condition had reversed and he was declining. Worse, it was now thought that he might be contagious and so all visiting was to be stopped.

"Surely that does not mean his family?" I asked, but the messenger didn't know the answer. Trying to hold off the panic which threatened to overwhelm me, I immediately sent a reply saying I was sure it did not apply to me. But an hour later a message came from James confirming that it did — to me especially, and Elizabeth and Frederick. Under no circumstances were we to go to St. James's Palace, and within it, Charles had been isolated in separate quarters. It was still unclear exactly what the problem was, but overnight Henry had deteriorated to the point of being conscious only part of the time. The doctors were retrying remedies, although they already had been without benefit.

"Do they mean there is nothing else they can do?" I asked Anna, as the possibility of Henry's dying became clear to me for the first time. "There must be something!"

But when instead of answering she turned her face away, I knew there was not. "God would not be so cruel as to take my son!" I exclaimed, still not wanting to believe it.

"God's ways are mysterious," was all she would say. I saw then that my women were crying. They had already heard the news from other sources, but had been unable to show they knew until I did.

"There is still hope," I said, despite being barely able to believe it. "We must all go to the chapel to pray."

The remaining hours of the day were spent mostly there, the chaplain leading us in prayer, interspersed with stretches of silence in which I waited for a divine reassurance that never came. That night I fell into a deep, empty sleep from which I woke after several hours, only to stare into the darkness. It was nearly impossible to imagine a world without Henry in it.

When morning finally came, it brought with it a new determination to see him. Out of everyone in our family, it mattered least if I should be taken by whatever illness he had, for what had been asked of me as queen had been accomplished, and if I died it would have little effect on anything. I decided to form a plan for entry into St. James's Palace. Directly after breakfast I sent for the Countess of Bedford to help me do so.

But when she arrived, she immediately told me not to proceed. "Elizabeth attempted the same yesterday," she said, "entering the part of the palace where Charles is, in disguise. Fortunately, Charles saw and recognised her, and had the good sense to stop her and return her to Whitehall. The king was beside himself when told. You must not now attempt the same. You would not succeed, and if the people found out it would agitate them. Already rumours of poison are spreading through London."

"Poison?" I asked in horror.

"We knew the prince has been ill for some time, but the people did not. For them this is sudden, and so they speculate. But the doctors do not believe it is that. Nor do I."

"What do you hear of Henry's condition?"

"Today should be decisive, one way or the other."

It would be almost unbearable to tolerate another day of the tension from such uncertainty. "This is James's fault! The Savoyard marriage is destroying Henry. I gave James the opportunity to retreat from it in front of him during the last visit, and he refused to take it. And Henry knew it."

"The king is despondent over this. He remains in his study and sees no one."

"As he usually does when troubled! He turns from everyone." Unexpectedly, and although I did not want to, I found myself sympathising with him. "This must be terrible for him," I said numbly.

"Perhaps it would help if we went to the chapel," the countess said.

The thought crossed my mind that it was those who had used religion for their own purposes, whether Catholic or Reformed, who had created a world that someone with the character of my son had found impossible to navigate.

But God, I thought, must still hear prayers that were simple and direct and without other motives. "Yes, to the chapel," I replied.

Something closed within me throughout the rest of the day, as each hour passed with no news. Somehow I slept through the night and maintained my composure the next day when news finally arrived that Henry's condition was now so hopeless James was leaving the city. As king and queen, we were not to attend the funeral. It was some sort of statement of continuity despite loss for the reassurance of the people, and there were indications that it was expected I would leave also. But I did not.

I stayed in my rooms, with Anna and the countess and my women. We were mostly silent, sitting by the windows and watching the ebb and flow of the Thames. And I was there when the following night the tolling of the bells all over the city told me Henry's life had ended.

19

Winter that year seemed endless, a long line of meaningless days where I stayed mostly secluded in my rooms in an attempt to push away the loss I could barely stand to think about. At least when alone, I was spared being reminded of it through the inadvertent comments of those around me. They had quickly learned not to speak directly of it to me after seeing I found no consolation in their reports of the outpouring of national grief at Henry's funeral, or of James's constant weeping while repeating his name. Almost everyone who came to see me was turned away. Obligatory visits from James and my other children were cold and formal and as brief as possible, during which I feared I might show my tendency to wonder why they were alive while Henry was not. At night my sleep, which I looked forward to all day, was deep but empty of dreams.

In February I participated in the ceremonies and festivities of Elizabeth's wedding as though playing a part in a masque. My mood was unchanged, even though I saw that the celebrations were helping the people of the country move past the shock of losing the prince on whom they had believed the future prosperity of the country had depended. There had been calls for the wedding to be cancelled, since Elizabeth's place in the succession had suddenly become so much more important, and people were reluctant for her to leave the country. But James had been adamant it should proceed after a short delay. Whether his reasons had been political, or from seeing the already deep attachment between Elizabeth and Frederick, I did not know. Dressed in finery I did what was expected of me, smiling and waving to the crowds with James and Charles at my side. But afterward I retreated to my rooms at Denmark House and put on one of my black mourning dresses again.

"The king won't like it," Anna said cautiously when she saw me doing so. "He declared that mourning would end with your daughter's wedding."

"Get out," I replied, "all of you." The women started to gather up the dress I had changed out of, but I told them not to. "Leave me!" I insisted, and they hurried out. I then sat in silence and stared at the dress on the chair where it had been left. It was beautiful, the Stuart colours of red and white, with gold embroidery. Then, I took it in my hands and tore it into as many pieces as I could, after which I stood at a window looking out onto the Thames. Its continuous flow, indifferent to the lives of those in the palaces and mansions alongside it, would no doubt go on for centuries.

I continued to wear black until April, when I learned I was required to go to Greenwich Palace, from where Elizabeth and Frederick would depart for Germany.

"It is time to put the mourning attire aside," Anna said.

"That is to be my decision alone," I replied dismissively.

But this time she stood her ground. "No, Your Majesty. It is time. Remember, the mother of Christ lost her son also. Yet, she went on."

I could barely believe she had said such a thing. "Go, leave me! And never say that to me again!"

She went out. But after I had spent a short while in my usual place, looking out at the Thames, I called her back. "Have my black dresses put away," I told her. "And please send a message to the king that after Greenwich, my taking the waters at Bath might be in order. Elizabeth's departure is another loss, and I might devolve into complete insanity if I return here afterward."

James agreed, and an extensive visit to Bath and surrounding areas was planned. I had little desire for it but knew it was necessary, in the same way that I had to be present at Greenwich in my usual clothing. As we made our preparations for the change of residence and following trip, I even felt a small, unfamiliar hope that, unlike during the wedding festivities, going through the motions of life as I had known it might feel right to me again, and effect a permanent change in my outlook.

But it did not. I arrived and settled into my rooms, but felt I was a stranger in the palace, staying somewhere for the first time. The others had already arrived and came to greet me, all offering indirect approval of my being out of mourning attire through compliments on my appearance. Their efforts, though, came to nothing. Almost immediately, I saw my attempts at involvement would be useless, and I retreated into the artificiality I'd assumed during the wedding. Henry's absence seemed absolutely impossible to accept.

"I cannot do this!" I told Anna as soon as we were alone. "We must return to Denmark House."

"No," she said. "You know you must continue trying."

"Do you think to tell me what I can and cannot do? You know nothing of what this has been to me! And I question whether you as a Catholic are not secretly pleased one who could have been a leader of the Reformed is gone!"

She looked as though I had struck her. "Your children are like mine, Your Majesty," she barely was able to say.

"Anna, I'm sorry, it was a terrible thing I said to you!" I reached out and grasped her wrist. "I still cannot make my way through this. Nothing feels the same. Everything is different."

There was a knock on the bedroom door. She opened it and let in one of my women, who told me the count was there, requesting to speak with me. "He is alone," she said. "The princess is not with him."

Frederick had visited with the others over the past months, but never alone, so the request was unusual. His presence had been of assistance during those visits, for I had almost no memories of him with Henry, although I had known of their respect and admiration for each other. His arrival now provided a distraction from my distress, and I agreed to see him. I would decide afterward whether or not to return to Denmark House.

His ability to speak and understand English had deepened significantly since last October, and he now greeted me in my reception room with self-assurance and ease. "Such a beautiful view onto the gardens," he said. "A change, for you, from the Thames."

The ever-flowing Thames had been my companion during the difficult past months, although its steadiness had provided little comfort. "These gardens are their finest now in spring," I answered, "when newly green."

"After the winter."

I'd been told he was subtle in intellect, and assumed he was now suggesting there would be a new spring for me. But I wasn't ready to accept it, and I moved away from him to the window. "What did you wish to speak to me about?" I asked, looking out.

He didn't answer, and when I turned back to him, I saw he wanted to tell me alone. I waved my hand so that the women in the room knew to leave, which they did.

"Elizabeth," he then said.

"Elizabeth?"

He came over to me, his handsome face becoming very serious in a way I had never seen before. "A matter troubles her peace of mind. I believe it must be resolved before we leave, so it can be left behind us, where it belongs. But I have been unable to convince her. I now think, most gracious Majesty and my mother, you are the only one who would be able to."

"What is it about?" I hoped it would be something minor, easily disposed of.

"Her brother," he answered without hesitation. "Henry." He then exhaled, as though it had been difficult to say it.

I turned away at once, startled to hear his name. "I cannot hear him spoken of!" I cried.

"Your Majesty —" he began.

"My son is dead and lost to us!" I nearly shouted as I took a step to leave the room.

"Your daughter lives," he replied steadily. "She blames his death on herself."

I stopped and looked back at him, surprised. "It was an illness that caused it. What are you saying?"

"She thinks herself responsible, in a way."

"How?" I asked incredulously.

"She says there was something else, that some invisible part of him was destroyed by the Savoy marriage the king wanted for him. That he could not come to terms with marriage with a Catholic. She says you knew it and tried to persuade her to marry Victor Emanuel to clear the way for a Reformed marriage for him. She wonders now if she should have."

Something within me pushed my own despair aside. "No! She must not think that!"

"She should not," he agreed. "But she does, sometimes. And since we now love each other, it is so difficult for me to hear. This was not so when I first arrived. We were not then in love. But as we came to be, it began to trouble her, as though she has no right to the joy which she has found, and he did not."

"Has she said she regrets her marriage to you?"

"No. But I can feel her thinking it. And I fear one day those thoughts might become such a regret."

"Frederick, I did approach her about reconsidering Victor Emanuel, and she is right as to why, although I know not how she came to understand my reason, for I never said it. Few knew it and would never have said so to her."

"It was unnecessary. She knew her father's ambition to bring balance to religion with his children's marriages. But since she could have married a Catholic with ease, she did not understand that it would have been so impossible for Henry."

"None of us did. I thought it was something he would dislike but eventually accommodate. My own understanding was inadequate. So was my response." It was terrible to acknowledge it, but I now knew that I too had failed.. But no matter how I felt, I had to be the mother my daughter needed. I had no doubt that Frederick was right in believing that I was the only one who could make a difference for Elizabeth.

"Where is she?" I asked. "There must be an end to this."

His face showed gratitude, and I felt it was yet another failure that he might have thought I wouldn't do whatever I could. But with my withdrawal into myself in the months since he had been here, he had not had an opportunity to see me differently. Fortunately, there was still time for me to show him I was not only a queen but a mother.

Elizabeth was in her suite, finishing the final arrangements for the English attendants who would be part of her retinue when they left. She looked surprised as I was announced and entered, as did everyone else in the room, who bowed and drew back to the sides.

"We must speak, daughter," I said as I reached her. "Alone." I sent the women who had accompanied me out with hers.

There was a tension about her, for she knew the visit was far from routine and not at all consistent with how I'd been for months. "I want only to set your mind at ease," I said as I took her hand and led her to a window seat.

She looked at me questioningly but said nothing as we sat.

"About Henry," I said, as though she had asked.

Her blue eyes closed and she leaned back against the frame of the window. "Frederick went to you," she said. "I am sorry he did. I'd thought he might, and I intended to tell him not to. I know the loss is still almost unbearable for you."

I held her hand between mine. "No, Elizabeth. It was good that he did. Barely in time, it seems, for what I am about to tell you certainly needed to be said before you leave. It may be years before we see each other again. And it is not something to be written in a letter."

She opened her eyes, and I was taken by their resemblance to Henry's. I said, "You and your brother looked so much alike; it was difficult at times to remember that in disposition you were so different. It was you who was blessed with the easier one, not always considering everything with such deep thought, or worrying how things might or might not turn out. It is something you should be grateful for, because it can make the difficulties of life smoother to navigate. It was how you made your decision to marry Frederick, and you made the right one. And it had no effect on what has happened to Henry."

She started to pull her hands away, but I didn't let her. "Elizabeth, it was illness that brought Henry where he is today. No matter what else we imagine or believe contributed to it, in the end, that is what it was. Frederick told me that you think, as I do, that he was deeply troubled by having a Catholic marriage. Perhaps had he not been, the illness never would have taken hold of him as it did. It is not something we are meant to know. But I can tell you I now believe that even if Henry had been given the Reformed marriage he wanted, he never would have found in it what you have already found in yours. Although I can almost not even say it, he was likely incapable of forming the same kind of bond."

She was staring at me as I continued, "My trying to interest you in Victor Emanuel was something I never should have done, and I am thankful I didn't succeed. You were right to set your own course, as we can now see. But I believe I should have continued trying to make your father understand how it was for a son who was so different from him. I didn't, for reasons I now have to accept. In the end, I still don't believe marriage would have brought Henry what your marriage has brought you. He didn't have the nature for it."

"A loving wife could have helped him find it," she said, but in a tone that was almost obligatory.

"I no longer believe that. And, my daughter, you do not have to, either. He wouldn't have wanted you to. Instead, take satisfaction that he so approved of your marriage. In your life, you accomplish what he believed he wanted. It continues through your going to live in the Palatinate and having children to take their places as leaders in the Reformed cause. That is how to respect the memory of him. Can you do that?"

The tension about her I'd seen when I'd come in was now gone. "Yes," she answered, "after such words of wisdom from you."

"Wisdom? It flatters me that you say it, but I don't think so. Instead, perhaps simple good sense. But I am not sure I even had that before now."

Something had fallen into place within me as I'd spoken to her. In showing her the beginning of a path for how to live without Henry, I'd also found one for myself. I would be eternally grateful to Frederick for having come to me, for not only had I helped my daughter but I had also reached a new understanding with her before she left. If she never saw me again, she would remember me so. And her departure would be bearable for me in ways that it might not have been before.

A few minutes later, when I left her, my women asked if I would return to my suite. I told them I would not, and then called Anna aside. "We are staying," I said, and she understood I had put away any thoughts of going to Denmark House instead. Then, I went in search of James.

He was in one of the rooms of his suite, on the opposite side from the door I came in through, with a crowd of courtiers between. When he heard me announced, he made his way through them and took my hand as he reached me. "Anne," he said, "how fine for you to be here. You have been missed."

Although I hadn't been sure of what I wanted to say to him, I'd intended to ask to speak to him alone. But as I stood there holding his hand, I felt differently. There had been a deep sincerity in what he had said to me, an acknowledgment that it had not been easy for me to appear at Greenwich at all. My presence alone was a statement that I was ready to move forward, and he recognised and appreciated it.

The doors I had entered through opened again, and Charles was announced and came in towards us. Then, almost immediately, Elizabeth and Frederick entered after him. And although I was still uncertain where the path ahead of me would lead, some of what would be on it was already clear.

HISTORICAL NOTE

In the following years, Anne became close to Charles, who was with her when she died in 1619. He became king after the death of James in 1625. Anne never saw Elizabeth again, who only returned to England briefly many years later. In the next century, Elizabeth's descendants succeeded to the British throne as the House of Hanover.

A NOTE TO THE READER

Dear Reader,

Thank you for reading *The Queen's Children*, the fourth in my series of novels about the Tudor and Stuart succession. It has the same narrator, Anne of Denmark, as my previous book, *The Queen's Cousin*, and continues the story of her family struggles after arriving in England, especially against the backdrop of the ongoing religious struggles of the time.

Like all the other books in this series, *The Queen's Children* is a novel, and not intended to present a full biographical portrait. My choices are always to select and creatively develop a particular strand, or perhaps a related few, of the many that make up a person's lifetime, that can fit within the structure of a novel. For this series, as I've stated elsewhere, those have been stories of royal women whose ambitions played out through their children, or their desires and ability to have them.

Although I had originally intended *The Queen's Cousin* and *The Queen's Children* to be one novel framed by the lifespan of Prince Henry, two distinct stories emerged, taking place at different times and in different locations, which I felt lent themselves to separate novels. I also always favor shorter novels for such serious and often tragic stories.

There is a wealth of biographical information about my subjects available on the internet, and I would encourage anyone seeking more knowledge about them to pursue their interest there. If you do, you'll find I have adhered to all reliable facts, especially dates and places. If you encounter any apparent difference, I suggest you search deeper, the way I have, into other sources.

I am always grateful for the interest of my readers, and enjoy reading their comments. If you liked *The Queen's Children*, or any of the others, I hope you'll post a review on Amazon and Goodreads.

Thank you!
Raymond Wemmlinger

Sapere Books is an exciting new publisher of brilliant fiction and popular history.

To find out more about our latest releases and our monthly bargain books visit our website:
saperebooks.com

www.ingramcontent.com/pod-product-compliance
Lightning Source LLC
Chambersburg PA
CBHW020610180626
46810CB00007B/2713